Forbidden Fruit

Ronda L. Caudill, PhD

Forbidden Fruit Copyright © 2013 Ronda L. Caudill, PhD

Published by Full Moon Publishing, LLC

ISBN-13: 978-0615819846
ISBN: 0615819842

Edited By Melissa Day
Cover Photography by Susan Stiltner
Cover models Nikita Caudill and Lindsay Stiltner
First Edition 2013

DEDICATION

This book is dedicated to Ricky, my wonderful husband who supports my every crazy idea and loves me no matter what. It is dedicated to my daughters Brittany and Nikita. Brittany is my beta reader who critiques my work and challenges me to make it better. Nikita gave me the idea for this book and pressed me to write it. I also would like to dedicate this book to my wonderful son-in-law, Travis, who is always there to lend a hand when I'm at my wits end and need technical support. I love you all. Thank you for all of your support and encouragement.

Ronda L. Caudill, PhD

Forbidden

Fruit

Ronda L. Caudill, PhD

Chapter 1

Lucinda Belle had always been a beautiful young woman—her internal beauty every bit as enchanting as her external beauty. Everyone was sure of Lucinda's goodness, purity and compassion. She always tried her best to help—family members, friends, strangers, and even animals. It was obvious to everyone that she received great pleasure from helping others. All who knew her loved her.

When Lucinda was a child, most of her loved ones succumbed to illness. Lucinda and one sister were the only children in her family to reach adulthood. Her father died when she was very young, and all her other siblings perished before she reached the age of fourteen. Her mother, Mary Belle, had no means to support them, so she did the only thing she could do. Mary went to work for a wealthy family, and she put Lucinda and her sister into service with other very wealthy families. She was devastated by having to separate her remaining family, but she had no other choice.

Mary Belle died at the age of forty, still in the service of the same wealthy family. Lucinda's sister, Francis, also stayed in the service of the same family she went to work for as a child, until she died a spinster at the age of fifty-one. Lucinda would, however, find her way into a new life. When she turned eighteen she left her employer's family after a very disturbing encounter with the master of the house, Judge Isaiah Whitman. The year was 1888.

Judge Whitman had always been a cruel man, and Lucinda avoided him at all costs. Lucinda always did as she was instructed by the judge, for fear of being dismissed and having no other place to go or, worse, of having to deal with his brutality. But on her eighteenth birthday she could take no more of his cruelty. His actions were more than Lucinda could bear.

Lucinda had gone into his study to dust. Judge Whitman was sitting at his desk, as usual. Lucida reached high upon a shelf to dust some old law books when the judge was suddenly behind her. Without warning, he reached out and grabbed her by the waist. The judge was stronger than Lucinda and she could not escape his grasp. He forced her to the floor. Before she knew what was happening, he had her long dress up around her waist. She fought trying to fend him off. The judge was brutal and forceful as he stifled Lucinda's screams with his large hand. Judge Whitman was a large man and, despite his prominent position, he always smelled of sweat, his teeth were bad, and his hair was always unkempt.

Before Judge Whitman could finish his brutal assault,

Lucinda brought her knee up hard into his groin causing him to release his grip on her.

He cried out through gritted teeth, "You'll regret this!"

With tears streaming down Lucinda's face like a great waterfall, she grappled with her clothing and ran from the room. She did not stop running until she was safely away from the house.

Lucinda took refuge in the back alleys of Whitechapel, having nowhere else to go. She had no idea where she would go or what she would do to survive. She only knew that she could not—and would not—go back to Judge Whitman. As night began to fall, Lucinda found a small, secluded area amongst a mound of crates behind the local pub. The alley was dark and smelled of urine and feces. Lucinda huddled up there in the filth to face the night alone. The night was sleepless and fretful.

Chapter 2

When day broke, Lucinda was frightened, hungry, and alone. As fate would have it, she would not stay that way for long.

Lucinda made her way down the alley back to the streets of Whitechapel. Upon arriving at the main street, Lucinda stumbled on her long, tattered, and dirty dress and fell into the path of an oncoming carriage. Little did she know, this was the carriage of the man who would change her life.

The coachman halted the horse just before it trampled Lucinda. The master of the carriage peered out the window to inquire of the driver what had happened. When he did, he saw Lucinda on the ground, her hands scraped and bloody from the fall. He hastily climbed from the carriage to check on the young lady.

The master of the carriage stooped down on one knee and held out his white-gloved hand to Lucinda. Her beautiful but tear-stricken face broke the kind man's heart. He knew he had to help her, no matter what her station in life was. She was the most beautiful woman he had ever laid eyes upon—thinly built, with silky dark hair, alabaster skin, rosy cheeks and lips, and emerald green eyes.

"Madam, I am so sorry. Please allow me to take you back to my home to launder your clothing and clean your wounds. That's the least I can do after we almost brought you to an end. What is your name?"

Lucinda looked up to find a handsome, distinguished man who appeared to be in his mid-thirties. His hair was dark and collar-length, and a little tussled. He had placid skin and warm, brown eyes. She could tell by the look in his eyes and the sound of his gentle voice that he was a man she could trust. She graciously accepted, "Thank you, kind sir. My name is Lucinda Belle."

As the master of the carriage helped Lucinda to her feet, he introduced himself as Dr. Aleister Wellington. "Come, I will help you into my carriage; I was on my way back to my home."

Lucinda let him assist her. "Thank you."

Once inside, Lucinda felt a strange, comforting feeling she had never before known.

Dr. Wellington offered grapes and wine to Lucinda. Lucinda ate and drank feverishly, having not eaten anything since early the day before. The ride was a bit longer than she had expected. The doctor's house was on the outskirts of town.

As they approached the house, Lucinda could not believe her eyes. It was the most beautiful mansion she had ever seen. It made the judge's house look like a commoner's home. Dr. Wellington's mansion was very large, made of stone, and had a wondrous turret on the front. The grounds in the front of the mansion were plush and inviting with a thick carpet of green.

The doctor admired Lucinda as her eyes widened at the sight.

Lucinda turned to the doctor, "Is this your home?"

"Yes, my lady. It is. Do you like it?"

"It is astounding, like nothing I have ever seen."

"Ms. Belle, you appear to be in some financial distress. May I open my doors to you until you can get on your feet? As you can see I have an abundance of room for guests. Will you accept my offer?"

"Sir, I don't know you. But, as I have no other choice but to go back to the streets, I accept your offer. Thank you."

Dr. Wellington's lips curled up slightly smiling kindly at Lucinda as they approached the gates. The carriage pulled up to the front door and halted beside a footman awaiting the doctor's arrival. The footman first took Lucinda's hand, treating her as someone of far greater status. He then assisted Dr. Wellington from the carriage.

Dr. Wellington took Lucinda's hand and led her into his beautiful home, where they were greeted by a woman he introduced as Ms. Poe, the head of his household staff. Ms. Poe was rather petite. She had grey hair pulled back tightly in a bun, her skin was shriveled and wrinkled, and her eyes were brown and kind. She made Lucinda immediately feel at ease.

"Ms. Poe, this is Lucinda Belle. She has fallen on hard times, so I have opened my doors to her until she can get back on her feet. Would you please see her to a room? See that she has a bath and find her some suitable clothing," Dr. Wellington instructed, as he handed his jacket and scarf to Ms. Poe.

"Yes, sir, of course," the housekeeper said. She took his things and hung them up in a nearby armoire. She then reached out and put her arm around Lucinda, guiding her away. "Come with me, child. Let's get you cleaned up and into some dry clothes. I'm sure you must be hungry, too."

Lucinda walked only a few steps and then turned to look at the man who had just saved her life, "Dr. Wellington, thank you so much. May God shine favor down upon you."

"Ms. Poe, stop for a moment," he commanded, with both authority and kindness. He walked over to Lucinda and took her dirty and bloody hand in his. He brought it up to his lips and kissed it. "You are very welcome, Ms. Belle. I hope you will tell me more about yourself. At dinner?"

"Of course, Sir," Lucinda said as he gently dropped her hand.

Dr. Wellington smiled at Lucinda and nodded to Ms. Poe as if to dismiss her. Ms. Poe curtseyed and then led Lucinda away and up the grand staircase.

Ms. Poe led Lucinda to a large room upstairs. It was beautifully decorated. In the center of the room was a large four-poster bed, with a huge canopy draped with beautiful blue silks. The other furnishings were equally exquisite. As beautiful as Judge Whitman's home was, it could not compare to this house.

"Ms. Belle, come over here and let's get you out of those rags," Ms. Poe said. She began to undress Lucinda. This was a switch for Lucinda. She had many times been where Ms. Poe was, helping a lady undress and prepare for a bath, but she had never been the one to be assisted. Ms. Poe rang a bell in Lucinda's room to alert other staff in the kitchen. Before Lucinda knew it, there were several maids in her room. Ms. Poe introduced Lucinda and instructed them to fill the large bathtub in Lucinda's room, secluded behind a moveable-dressing screen.

Lucinda felt humbled by the attention. She felt like she hadn't done anything in her life to deserve such treatment. She would have been happy with a pitcher of cold water and a bowl. She never expected such lavish treatment.

The ladies filled the tub with hot water, sprinkled with lavender oil to give it a lovely fragrance. Once she was undressed, two maids took Lucinda's hands and helped her step into the steaming tub of water.

Lucinda's skin tingled beneath the warmth of the water. Lucinda could never remember ever having a warm bath before.

Ms. Poe then instructed the other maids to find a gown and some undergarments for Lucinda. They left while Ms. Poe washed Lucinda from top to bottom, careful when cleaning her skinned hands.

"Oh, dear, you should be happy it was the good doctor that happened upon you. It is by the grace of God that you are here with us. He is a good man and will make sure you are cared for and safe," she said to Lucinda.

"It is curious. Why did he have mercy upon me and bring me here?" Lucinda asked.

"Well, he is a good man. If he happens upon someone in need, he feels it is his duty to help. He wasn't always blessed. He came from very meager means. His family died when he was very young. He was on his own at a very young age. Grace favored him once, too. He was found in the streets by a doctor's wife. She was barren and had no children. She fell in love with him the minute she saw him. He was starving and sick—on the verge of death, I've been told. The doctor's wife took him in and gave him a home and an education. He then vowed to return the favor whenever and to whomever he could. And he has," Ms. Poe explained.

"What of his real family. Does he remember them?" Lucinda inquired.

"Well, that is a bit of a mystery. He doesn't like to talk about them, but he has confided in me a time or two. His mother was a prostitute and his father was a brutal drunkard. He witnessed untold things as a child—things he will not discuss. That's all he has ever told me. He revealed this to me when his adoptive mother died. He needed someone to talk to, and I was there. We have a special bond. He feels more like a son than a master to me."

Ms. Poe helped Lucinda out of the bath and dried her. She rang the bell again and the others came back with the most beautiful clothes Lucinda had ever seen. They assisted Lucinda with her corset, pulling it as tight as they could. Lucinda had never worn one. She was but a maid herself, and never had the need or opportunity to wear one. She was pulled, tugged, and squeezed until she fit perfectly into the amazing gown provided for her.

When they had finished dressing her, they began to work on her hair. They then dressed her wounds. Just when she thought they had finished, she heard a knock at the door. It was Dr. Wellington. Ms. Poe answered the door. Lucinda could not hear what was said, but when Ms. Poe shut the door, Lucinda could not believe her eyes. Dr. Wellington had brought up a beautiful necklace for Lucinda to wear to diner.

Ms. Poe proceeded toward Lucinda. "This was his mother's. I have never before seen it out of its box. You must have really touched his heart. Here, my dear," Ms. Poe said, as she clasped the necklace around Lucinda's neck. It was a beautiful emerald necklace that matched her eyes. It caught the light shining in through the window and sparkled brightly.

"I can't wear this. It's too exquisite."

"You mustn't deny the master of his wishes. He asks very little of us," Ms. Poe insisted.

"Very well."

Ms. Poe told Lucinda to wait in her room until dinner. Lucinda complied. She sat by the window in a large plush chair and cast her eyes about the grounds. They were beautifully kept. There was a labyrinth of hedges, with benches, trees, and flowers. There was also an abundance of statues and fountains about the grounds.

Just as Lucinda began to daydream—that this was her home and that she was the lady of the house—she heard a knock at the door.

"Yes?" Lucinda called out.

Ms. Poe opened the door and entered the room. "Dinner is served, my dear. Follow me, please."

Lucinda stood and followed Ms. Poe to the dinning hall. Dr. Wellington was already seated at the head of the table. He stood to greet Lucinda, and as he stood, he had to do a double take. He could not believe what he saw. He had thought this young woman was beautiful when she was dirty and in rags, scratched and bruised. But she was breathtaking now, cleaned and in a gown.

"Ms. Belle. Thank you for joining me. I trust you are feeling a bit better?" Dr. Wellington asked.

"Yes, much. Thank you. This necklace, though, it's too much. I really shouldn't be wearing it. It might become lost or damaged."

"I trust that you are a capable young woman. I think it will be safe around your neck for a few hours. Besides, it looks beautiful on you. Please, humor me," he said, as he pulled her chair out.

"If you insist."

"Thank you," he said, as he took his seat. Their meal was served and they talked, getting to know one another. Dr. Wellington did not reveal much about his past before Dr. and Mrs. Wellington had taken him in. Lucinda, however, hid nothing from him. She told him everything about her life— how most of her family had died, how she had gone into service at the home of Judge Whitman, how the judge had tired to take liberties with her against her will, and how she had narrowly escaped and ran away—everything up to the point where she fell in front of his carriage.

Dr. Wellington was saddened for the life that Lucinda had lived. He was appalled at Judge Whitman's actions. But then, too, in the back of his mind, he was also thankful, because otherwise he would never have met Lucinda. Dr. Wellington didn't know quite what to say, only that he was sorry for her lifetime of misfortune and heartache. He then said, "Here is to a new life, to future joys," as he held up his wine-filled glass as a toast.

Lucinda couldn't help but feel that, maybe if only for an instant, she could be happy. She raised her glass and joined in the toast, "To a new life." And she had the overwhelming urge to smile.

"Ms. Belle, you should really smile more often. You have a lovely smile," Dr. Wellington said.

Lucinda quietly replied, "I have not had a lot to smile about until today."

"I hope you mean because of me."

"Yes, thank you for your kindness and generosity. For the first time in my life, I feel like smiling."

"I hope I can make you smile much more in the future."

Lucinda looked a bit uncomfortable with Dr. Wellington's comment, not knowing exactly how to take it. She didn't respond, she only averted her eyes from him and bowed her head. Dr. Wellington could see Lucinda's discomfort, so he rang the bell on the table beside his plate. Almost immediately, one of the maids entered the room.

"Yes, sir," she responded, as she bowed her head and curtseyed.

"We are ready for dessert, please."

"Yes, sir. Right away." And the maid disappeared. Moments later, she reappeared with cake.

"Thank you," Dr. Wellington said as they were served.

Lucinda had never had such a delightful meal. But she almost regretted it. If she were never to have another of its equal, she would never have known what she had been missing. Now, that innocence was forever gone. It was almost like the forbidden fruit in the Garden of Eden. She would never again be satisfied with common food and the scraps she was used to.

They finished their meal. Dr. Wellington excused himself and retired for the night. Lucinda went up to her room. She wondered how she would ever undress by herself.

Lucinda removed the necklace and placed it upon the dressing table. She then removed her shoes. And as she was taking the pins from her hair a soft rap came at her door.

"Ms. Belle, may I come in?" the familiar voice of Ms. Poe asked.

"Yes, Ms. Poe. Please come in." Lucinda was quite happy Ms. Poe was there.

"Oh, dear. Look at you, still in your gown. Let me help you. The master told me you had finished dining; I thought I would check on you," she told Lucinda, as she moved closer and coaxed Lucinda from her chair.

Ms. Poe began to methodically unbutton and unlace, and finally was able to free Lucinda from her gown and her bustier. She took the gown and hung it in the armoire. She walked over to a nearby dresser and pulled out a beautiful white silk nightgown. "Here you go, Ms. Belle. You will be much more comfortable in this." Ms. Poe assisted Lucinda with the nightgown.

"Please, Ms. Poe, call me Lucinda. I am but a commoner, no better than you or anyone else."

"I have to disagree with you on that. If Dr. Wellington saw something special about you and he calls you Ms. Belle, why should I call you Lucinda? But if you insist, in private I will call you Lucinda, but not in the presence of Dr. Wellington," Ms. Poe reluctantly agreed.

"Thank you."

"Okay then, Lucinda. I will take my leave. Try to get some rest. I must warn you, though; at times, this house feels as though it takes on a life of its own. Don't be frightened; just stay in here and you will have nothing to fear." Ms. Poe turned to walk away.

"Ms. Poe, what do you mean?"

"The house just creaks and moans, and seems very lonely and sad at night. That's all. Just stay here until I come for you in the morning."

"Ms. Poe, do you know what Dr. Wellington has planned for me? Does he intend to eventually turn me out or put me to work, or does he have something entirely different in mind?"

Ms. Poe smiled and replied kindly, "Don't worry, child. Whatever he has planned for you, I'm certain it's in your best interest. He will not put you in harm's way. He has brought you here, and he will make sure to care for you."

"But why? I am a total stranger of meager means—a peasant."

"He is a good man and was moved to do good. You are not the only one he has ever helped. He does what he can, when he can, to help whomever he can. It's time for sleep; no more questions tonight. Goodnight." Ms. Poe left the room and closed the door behind her.

Lucinda was quite tired from the day's events, and satisfied from her wonderful meal. She lay down in that warm, cozy bed and sleep came soon.

She had not been asleep long before she heard a noise from outside her door. It sounded like scratching. She wondered what could be making such a sound. She remembered Ms. Poe's warning about not leaving the safety of her room, but curiosity got the better of her. She arose from her bed and lit a bedside lamp. She picked up the lamp and made her way to the door. She opened it slowly. The creaking of the door made her shudder.

Lucinda looked up and down the hall, but saw nothing out of the ordinary. She turned to go back into her room to bed, but heard scratching again. She turned quickly but there was nothing there. The scratching continued. Lucinda had a morbid sense of curiosity and could not turn away from a mystery or even terror. She had to investigate, no matter what she might find.

She called out, "Is there someone there? Do you want something of me?"

There was no answer. She called out again and began to walk away from her room. She walked slowly looking around every corner. Eventually Lucinda made her way downstairs to the entrance hall. Still, she saw no one. Then, when she had satisfied herself that there was nothing to be found, she turned to make her way back to her room. When she turned, she saw a shadow move across the room in front of the window.

"Is there anyone here?"

No reply. She walked to the other side of the room. Before she could make her way to the window, she heard, "Ms. Belle! What are you doing in here?"

She turned with a start to find Dr. Wellington, standing in his nightshirt behind her.

"I'm sorry," Lucinda apologized, "I thought I heard something outside my room and I was seeking to find it."

"Ms. Belle, were you not instructed by Ms. Poe to stay

in your room until morning?" Dr. Wellington gruffly asked.

"Yes, sir."

"Then you should heed her warning. Now, please go back to your room," he instructed.

"But I think you should check that window."

"Ms. Belle, I must insist you go back to your room, now," he scolded.

"Of course, Dr. Wellington. I'm very sorry. I beg your forgiveness. Goodnight," Lucinda started to walk by him, and he grabbed her lightly by the arm.

"I don't mean to sound unkind, but it's really for your own safety. It is a big house and we are quite far out. There could be an intruder. I will check. But first, let me see you safely back to you room."

"That's really not necessary."

"Please, Ms. Belle. For my peace of mind."

"As you wish, sir," Lucinda conceded.

Dr. Wellington took her lamp, took her hand, and led her back to her room. "Ms. Belle, please lock your door when I take my leave, and don't open it until the cock's crow.

Please."

"I will do as you say. Thank you again for your hospitality. Goodnight, Dr. Wellington."

"Goodnight, Lucinda Belle." He handed her the lamp and turned. He walked out the door and disappeared down the long corridor in the dark. But his voice echoed back, "Ms. Belle, close and lock that door."

Without a word, Lucinda did as she was instructed. But her sleep was restless that night. She couldn't understand why she must be sequestered to her room behind a looked door. Does everyone else have to abide by this rule? And why? Her thoughts raced with the possibilities. Was there something hideous that came out after dark? Was there a tendency for intruders? Was Dr. Wellington fearful of her falling and injuring herself? Or was he hiding a secret that he was afraid might be exposed? Lucinda couldn't help but to be a little suspicious.

Lucinda finally fell asleep in the early morning hours. It felt as though she had just closed her eyes when she heard a knock at the door.

"Yes? Ms. Poe?"

"Can you let me in? I need to get you dressed.

Breakfast is prepared and Dr. Wellington insists on having you dine with him for breakfast."

"Yes, of course. I'm sorry," Lucinda said, as she scrambled to her feet and rushed to unlock the door.

Ms. Poe reached into the armoire and retrieved another beautiful gown, though not quite as elegant as the one from the night before. "Here, let's get you presentable." Ms. Poe ushered Lucinda from her nightgown quickly, and with great haste and purpose. She sat Lucinda down and brushed her hair, pinning it up in a conservative manner. "Now you are ready. Follow me, please."

"Ms. Poe, what about the necklace?" Lucinda pointed to the necklace Dr. Wellington had insisted she wear the night before.

"I will retrieve it and return it to its place while you dine with the doctor. Now, come."

Ms. Poe rushed down the hall, down the stairs and into the kitchen, pulling Lucinda by the hand. Just before the entrance to the dining hall, Ms. Poe stopped and adjusted Lucinda's dress and hair. "Now, then. Go on in. He's waiting for you." Ms. Poe gave Lucinda a slight push through the entrance.

"Ah, good morning, Ms. Belle," Dr. Wellington greeted Lucinda.

"Dr. Wellington." Lucinda curtseyed and then seated herself.

"Ms. Belle, I have thought about it and have decided to offer you a permanent home here, if you would like. I can offer you an education in etiquette, and social status, among other things."

"Dr. Wellington, you have to know that I would be suspicious of your motives," Lucinda stated plainly.

Dr. Wellington laughed, put his fork down, and wiped his mouth with his napkin. "Well, you see, Ms. Belle, there is a belief that I hold to be true: karma. Are you aware of the term?"

"Yes, I can read. I have come across the term. It basically means that what you do comes back to you, whether it be good or bad."

"Yes, ma'am, that's exactly what it means. In my life, my adoptive parents did many wonderful things for me, taking me off the streets and raising me as their own. I have had a good life and much luck since then. So you see, Ms. Belle, I feel it is my duty to return good fortune to those I can help. I try to do it as often as possible. I believe you found me so I can help you. In return, I hope you will do this for others in need. It's that simple. Will you accept my offer?"

"This all makes sense. But are you sure you want to take on the responsibility of providing for a total stranger?"

"There is not a doubt in my mind. I think you have a lot to offer this world, if you had the opportunity. So, what is your answer? Will you accept?"

"Well, I have no other place to go, and the possibility of finding new work seems little to none."

Dr. Wellington smiled. "No, and I don't think the good judge is thinking very highly of you right now, so I'm certain you no longer have a position there."

Lucinda smiled slightly, "I guess not. So I will accept your offer. However, I will not take charity. You must let me repay you in some way. I am very skilled in cooking, cleaning, sewing, gardening, and other talents."

"Ms. Belle, I would like for you to be educated, and then we will see how you may repay me. I can see you are indeed a very proud woman. Pride can often be one's worst enemy, though. Please, do not let it be yours."

"I must insist on some type of repayment after my education is complete."

"Very well. Now, I must have a party to celebrate the newest member of this house."

"That's really not necessary. Why, pray tell, would you want to put a poor servant girl on display?"

"Ms. Belle, you are much more than a poor servant girl. You have much potential. If you are going to be educated and become a part of high society, then you need an introduction. You need to be accustomed to mingling with the socialites of London."

"As you wish. Thank you."

After Dr. Wellington and Lucinda finished breakfast, he asked to escort her through his beautiful, lavish, English gardens. As they walked, she was amazed at the beauty of Dr. Wellington's home, gardens, and demeanor. He finally escorted her back into the house. Their stroll was not extensive; the doctor had work that day.

"Ms. Belle, I really hate to, but I must go into town to work. I am already late. But I wanted to make certain you accepted my proposal. Now that I have that peace of mind, I will carry on my day as usual. I will take my leave and see you upon my return tonight." Dr. Wellington turned to depart, but after a few steps he pivoted on his heels and said, "Ms. Belle, Ms. Poe will assist you in anything you may require. Just call upon her."

"Thank you, doctor," Lucinda said as she curtseyed. He smiled, turned and left.

Lucinda wasn't sure what to conclude from the morning's events. She wasn't certain how she would fill her day.

Lucinda wandered about the stately mansion, exploring. No one had informed her that any place was off limits. So, she decided to explore as much of the house as possible.

After a few hours, Ms. Poe found Lucinda. "Lucinda, I have been searching everywhere for you, child."

"I'm sorry. No one said I couldn't explore. I was just curious," Lucinda said apologetically.

"Oh, we don't mind your curiosity. But I need you to be fitted for dresses. Dr. Wellington, doesn't ask much of us, but when he does have a specific request, he expects it to be carried out." Ms. Poe gently tugged at Lucinda's arm, pulling her toward the massive staircase.

"I don't need tailored dresses. Why does he want me fitted?"

"Well, you'll need dresses to wear when you are away at Lady Kingston's Etiquette School for Young Women."

Lucinda was astonished. She had just come to terms with being taken in by the good doctor. She didn't expect to be sent away to school. She had assumed she would be schooled at the doctor's home. She didn't relish the idea of being sent away; she felt very comfortable at the house. Everyone was kind to her. How would she be treated at Lady Kingston's? She new that the Whitman's daughter, Victoria attended Lady Kingston's as well as many of the wealthy young women of London.

"I'm being sent away? When? Why? Etiquette school will be very expensive. It's really not necessary." Lucinda protested.

"Lucinda, as I said before, the good doctor asks very little of us. If he wants you to attend etiquette school, then that is what you should do. You really can't argue with him. He has a way of coercing one to his will. There is no use arguing or resisting. Just come with me and be fitted."

"Very well," Lucinda said, feeling defeated.

They reached Lucinda's room, where they met a seamstress, several maids, and many bolts of exquisite material—silk, satin, velvet, and lace. Lucinda had never before seen such beautiful material.

"Oh my, these dresses will be terribly expensive. Are you sure I should accept them?"

"Lucinda, stop fighting the inevitable." Ms. Poe began to undress Lucinda, as the seamstress retrieved her tape measure, pins, scissors and thimble from her bag.

Lucinda finally gave in, deciding it was hopeless to go against the wishes of Dr. Wellington. However disappointed she was about having to leave, she knew she would have to give in.

Lucinda spent most of the day with the seamstress, with the exception of taking lunch. That night she dined alone; Dr. Wellington did not come home to dine with her as he had said he would. He did not return until after she had already retired for the night. According to Ms. Poe, this was not an unusual occurrence.

Chapter 3

Judge Whitman was certain Lucinda would be back. He was very surprised when she did not return. He had assumed she would eventually come back, groveling on hands and knees. His wife, Melinda, was very fond of Lucinda and was disappointed to discover that she had disappeared. She couldn't imagine what made Lucinda leave. After all, Lucinda had been with them for years. She seemed satisfied.

Life went on as usual at the judge's home. Judge Whitman called upon his wife to find a replacement for Lucinda. Melinda thought it all but impossible to find a replacement for Lucinda, such a hard and obedient worker. But she did as her husband had asked and began to inquire.

The judge left early the day after Lucinda's disappearance. He arrived at his office and conducted his workday as usual. Then, he received an unlikely visitor, an acquaintance he had not spoken to in months, Dr. Wellington.

"Judge Whitman," Dr. Wellington greeted him.

"Doctor, to what do I owe this honor?" Judge Whitman extended his hand to Dr. Wellington.

Dr. Wellington shook his hand and took a sit across the

desk from the judge. "Well, actually I have recently taken in a young lady. I am having a ball to welcome her and introduce her to the socialites of England. I wanted to invite you and your lovely wife and daughter. I understand that your daughter attends Lady Kingston's."

"That's right."

"This particular young lady will be attending Lady Kingston's Etiquette School as well. I thought it would be nice if she knew someone before arriving at the school. I also wanted to introduce her to everyone of importance. So, will you do me the honor and attend?"

Judge Whitman, knowing the stature and utter importance the good doctor had in the community, accepted eagerly. "Of course, it would be my honor. Thank you for thinking of us. Just send me the invitation and we will be there."

"Very well then. Thank you." Dr. Wellington turned and left Judge Whitman's office.

Judge Whitman couldn't wait to tell his wife and daughter the news. He went back to his work and finished his day early so he could give them the news.

Dr. Wellington, however, stayed at his office longer

that night. He, after all, had some business to attend to—business that others would not understand. A couple of times a week, he would receive visits from grave robbers who would bring him fresh cadavers. The good doctor would cut open the cadavers methodically and examine them. He would perform experiments in a secret underground laboratory that would rival that of Dr. Victor Frankenstein. He never wanted Lucinda to discover this part of his life; he feared she would not understand his reasons.

That night, he received a special specimen. The grave robbers brought him a man who had two additional appendages—arms. The man had been a member of a traveling circus, which had come through town, when he was killed by an elephant. No one had claimed the body, and the circus had moved on. The town put him in a cheap pine box in a shallow grave. The grave robbers knew Dr. Wellington would pay good money for such a find—they wasted no time.

Dr. Wellington was so fascinated with the corpse that he lost all track of time and was later than usual getting home. When he did arrive home, he went straight to Lucinda's room to make sure she had remembered to lock her door. To his dismay, she had again ignored his request—a most important request.

He looked in on her. He admired her beauty for only a moment, then he promptly left, locking the door behind him with the master key. As he proceeded to his room, he heard the unmistakable scratching sound that disturbed him so frequently. Dr. Wellington stopped momentarily to see if he could locate the source of the noise. He didn't see anything. Other nights, he had seen an ungodly shadow with the scratching sound. Not tonight. He reached his room and retired shortly thereafter.

The remainder of the night passed much too quickly, and he was awakened the next morning by Ms. Poe knocking at his door and calling out to him.

"Dr. Wellington, are you alright? It's nearly ten. We have already had breakfast and have begun our day. Dr. Wellington?"

Dr. Wellington answered with a groggy voice, "Yes, Ms. Poe. My work kept me out later than I had anticipated. I will see you in a few minutes. Would you please heat my breakfast and ask Ms. Belle to join me?"

"Yes, sir. Of course."

As Dr. Wellington prepared for breakfast, Ms. Poe found Lucinda in the gardens. Lucinda had discovered a special spot that set her mind at ease. It was a secluded place in the midst of the labyrinth of hedges, on a bench by a breathtaking statue of the goddess Aphrodite.

"Lucinda, come with me. Make haste, Dr. Wellington is waiting on you."

"What does he want with me? I would have thought he was already at his office. I didn't realize he was still here," Lucinda questioned.

"He wants you to sit with him whilst he has his breakfast." Ms. Poe once again ushered Lucinda by the elbow, in the direction of the house.

"But why?"

"I don't know. I don't question his requests; I just carry them out. Now come," Ms. Poe insisted.

"Very well." Lucinda picked up her pace. She was extremely curious why Dr. Wellington wanted her to sit with him.

Dr. Wellington had arrived at the table in the dining hall just before Lucinda and Ms. Poe. He looked up and Lucinda's beauty made his heart skip a beat.

"Good morning, Ms. Belle."

"Good morning, Dr. Wellington," Lucinda said, as he stood and pulled out a chair for her.

"I trust you slept well."

"I did. Thank you."

"No more nightly strolls?"

"No," Lucinda smiled.

"You must remember to lock your bedroom door when you retire. When I came in last night, I checked on you and locked it," he scolded.

Lucinda was curious why he would feel the need to check her door. "I will try to remember from now on."

"Please do. I wouldn't want you to meet with an unfortunate accident in the night and have no one be aware."

"Of course. You're right."

"Now, on to other business. I got in very late last night and have not had the chance to speak with Ms. Poe about your fittings yesterday. I trust that went well—to your liking." He leaned back slightly to receive his plate from one of the staff. He picked up his fork and began to devour his breakfast.

"It was fine. I just don't think it was necessary. The material was quite exquisite and, I'm sure, very expensive. I would be just as happy in dresses made of more humble material."

"Did Ms. Poe not explain to you that you would need the best for Lady Kingston's Etiquette School?"

"She did explain that I would need them for etiquette school—but she did not mention they should be the best. Why would they need to be so lavish?"

"Lucinda Belle, you have accepted my hospitality—I now consider myself your benefactor. Now, you can ask anyone who knows me and they will say that anyone or anything in my charge receives only the best quality. My house, my horses, my gardens—now you."

"You speak of me as a possession. I did not accept any such terms."

"Ms. Belle, you misunderstand me. I didn't mean to categorize as a possession. I was just pointing out that my standards are high. If I am your benefactor, then you should receive no less than my possessions. You are a person—your own person."

"Why must I go away to be educated in etiquette? I can

just as easily be educated here," Lucinda protested in vain.

"Because I am your benefactor, and Lady Kingston's provides the best education in etiquette for young women. Again, I provide only the best."

"Well, then, if that is your wish, I will oblige you and thank you once again for your generosity."

Dr. Wellington continued to eat. Lucinda wandered why he was out so late and where had he been. He had said he would dine with her the night before and then did not. The uncomfortable silence and her curiosity got the best of her, and she finally had to ask.

"Dr. Wellington, can I ask you a question—a question I am certain is none of my business—but may I be so bold?"

"You can ask me anything. However, I won't promise to divulge the answer."

"Well, you didn't return home until after everyone had retired for the night. I asked Ms. Poe about it; she said it was not unusual for you to work late a few nights a week. Why? What is that you do so late, and where?"

"Ms. Belle, you are taking great liberties asking such questions. I should say that I am the master of this house, and it is absolutely none of your concern. However, I like your boldness and your inquisitiveness. So, I will honor you with a partial answer. I have a laboratory that very few are aware of. I would appreciate discretion on that fact."

"Of course. Anything you tell me is kept in the utmost confidence. I will not share any of our conversations with anyone."

"Thank you. I appreciate that. Well, you see, in this laboratory I conduct scientific experiments that are not accepted by society, but are imperative to the progression of medicine. I can't very well carry out such experimentations during business hours, where someone may discover my actions."

"I understand completely. So, you examine corpses?" Lucinda said matter-of-factly.

Dr. Wellington smiled.

"Ms. Belle, you really amaze me. How unaffected by such an admission. Most women would have fainted at the mere prospect of such an act."

"I am not naive and innocent. I have seen my share of atrocities. My life has not been jaded. Nothing surprises me, doctor."

"To answer your question, yes, I examine corpses."

"How do you come by them? Grave robbers?"

"I do have dealings with some unscrupulous individuals. Let's leave it at that, shall we?"

"Of course. I now have an admission to make, if you would like to hear it."

"I am all ears, Ms. Belle. My curiosity is now piqued." Dr. Wellington sat straight up in his chair, anxiously awaiting Lucinda's revelation.

"I was once poor—very poor—and had to do unspeakable things just to survive. For a brief time, just before I went into service with Judge Whitman, I was associated with a couple of grave robbers. I assisted them in obtaining and delivering a few bodies to a doctor or two myself."

Dr. Wellington could not believe what Lucinda had just confessed to him. "Well, then, Ms. Belle, you have surprised me, I think, more than I surprised you. Next time, I won't be so concerned about your opinion of me."

"Was that too much information, too soon?"

"Not at all. In fact, it gives me a sense of relief,

knowing that you don't judge me." Dr. Wellington wiped his mouth and pushed his chair back from the table. "Shall we take a walk to the stables? You haven't seen my horses."

"I don't feel the need to judge. And yes, I would like to take a walk to the stables. I love horses."

He pulled out her chair and laced her arm through his. They walked to the stables. Lucinda enjoyed being with Dr. Wellington; he was genuinely kind and pleasant to be around. When he took her in, she wasn't certain of his motives and she still wasn't certain about anything, but she was beginning to trust him. And she had trusted so few in her life.

The sun was bright and the dew had already dried. It was a brisk but pleasant day. Lucinda enjoyed the outdoors; she had so little time to spend outside while she was in the service of the judge. She speculated that she been outside more in the few days she had been with Dr. Wellington than during her entire stay at the Whitman's.

Lucinda enjoyed the warmth of the sun beating upon her shoulders and the scent of the fresh morning air. A nearby stream gave a serene sound. The entire estate gave a sense of relaxation and peacefulness—except at night. The first night had unnerved Lucinda, and she couldn't understand why Dr. Wellington was so adamant about keeping the doors locked at night.

Lucinda enjoyed the walk so much; it seemed no time before they reached the stables. She was amazed to see so many beautiful horses. She was also amazed to see how much they liked Dr. Wellington.

"Well, do you like them?" Dr. Wellington asked proudly.

Lucinda walked over and caressed the ears of a solid black mare. "Yes, they are breathtaking."

"Her name is Lady Jane. Do you like her?"

"She is spectacular."

"She seems to like you." They strolled about the stables and visited all of the horses.

"Well, Ms. Belle, we should probably head back now."

He took her by the arm as they walked back to the house. Dr. Wellington did not go to work in town that day. Instead, he entertained visitors—business associates, Lucinda reckoned. He disappeared into his office and Lucinda did not see him for the remainder of the day. Once again, she dined alone.

After she had dinner, Ms. Poe showed Lucinda to her room and helped her undress. "Remember to lock this door. Dr. Wellington reprimanded me for not ensuring your safety last night."

"I will, but why? What is so important that I should be barricaded in my room throughout the night? Is there something evil here?"

"I am not at liberty to tell you why you should keep your door locked. Just know that we all do, and there is a good reason. Now, get into bed." Ms. Poe walked to the door. "Lucinda, please lock this door first."

Lucinda did as was requested and locked the door behind Ms. Poe. She extinguished her bedside lamp and got into bed. Lucinda fell into a restless sleep, hearing several strange noises. Lucinda heard scuffling feet pacing just outside her bedroom. She sat up in her bed to listen more closely. She was surprised to see light shining under the crack of the door, and shadows passing back and forth. She wondered who could be there and why.

Lucinda slipped from her bed and crept across the room without a sound. The shadow and the scuffling noise were still present. She turned the key in the lock slowly, careful not to make a sound. She took hold of the doorknob and pulled the door open quickly, certain she would discover who was there. The hall was vacant. The candles in the sconces outside her bedroom were lit, but the shadow had vanished. There was no one and nothing there. She slammed the door shut and locked it. She ran and jumped back into her bed, full of fear. Lucinda heard the pacing sound and saw the shadows once again. She did not get up again to see what it was. She lay there, dozing in restless slumber, with whatever it was pacing outside her door all night.

Lucinda awoke groggily to the sound of Ms. Poe knocking at her door. "Lucinda. Lucinda, are you awake?"

"Yes, Ms. Poe," Lucinda said, her voice barely audible.

"May, I come in?"

"Yes, of course." Ms. Poe let herself in with a master key.

"Dear, you look terrible. Are you ill?" Ms. Poe walked over and opened the drapes, letting brilliant morning sunlight beam across the room, directly into Lucinda's sleep-deprived eyes.

Lucinda reached up to cover her eyes.

Ms. Poe turned to see the discomfort her actions had

caused. "Oh my." She drew the drapes enough to keep the sun from shining in Lucinda's face. She walked over, and sat on the side of Lucinda's bed. Ms. Poe reached over and put her wrist on Lucinda's forehead. "You're not feverish. What is it, dear?"

"Ms. Poe, you wouldn't believe me if I told you."

"Try me."

"You'll think me mad. I am beginning to question my own sanity." And then, Lucinda told Ms. Poe of the last night's strange events. "Do you think I lost all my senses?"

"No, my dear. There are many questionable goings on in this big old house. I have seen and heard things that are unexplainable."

"Has Dr. Wellington?"

"Yes, we all have. This is why he wants us sequestered to our rooms at night. He thinks this will keep us safe. And so far, it has."

"Does he know what it is?"

"If he does, he hasn't shared such information with us—only that we should stay locked in our rooms for our own safety."

"Shall I ask him?"

"If you wish. I don't know that he would tell you, though. Now, on to other things. We must have you fitted for yet another gown—one for the ball."

Lucinda once again did not see Dr. Wellington until dinner. He had left before she awoke and, when he arrived home, stayed in his room until dinner was served. Nevertheless, Lucinda had set her mind to ask him what was going on with the house.

Chapter 4

Dr. Wellington was restless that night, hearing pacing outside his door. He was unaware the same occurrence was happening outside Lucinda's door. He finally gave up on sleep just before dawn. He arose early and went into town. He decided to go down into his laboratory to work before he saw patients.

He had an open cadaver on the examining table. Dr. Wellington cut and carved, examining the muscle tissue, the heart, and the lungs. He opened the skull, removing the brain for future examination. He stored it in a large jar of curing solution and sealed the jar tightly. Finally, it was time to accept patients. He locked the laboratory and ascended the darkened steps to his office.

He saw a few patients, and then called for an assistant to deliver invitations for the upcoming ball. The good doctor continued his work. When the day was finally at an end, he returned home. He had been looking forward to the time he would spend with Lucinda. He had grown very fond of her in the few short days he had spent with her.

He was met by Ms. Poe at the door. "Good evening, sir. Let me take your things." She took his coat, hat and gloves.

"What is it, Ms. Poe? You only meet me at the door if you have an issue."

"It's Ms. Belle, sir."

"Is she alright? What is it?"

"Oh, no, sir. She's just fine. She was fitted for the ball gown today, per your request. It's just that she had an encounter last night. She's been asking questions."

"It was inevitable. I was hoping it would be a little later. But I guess I must deal with this straight away."

"That would be best. She mentioned that she might ask you about it this evening at dinner."

"Very well, all will be revealed at the table tonight. Thank you, Ms. Poe." The good doctor went into his room until dinner.

At dinnertime, Lucinda came down to the dining hall. She was seated at the table. Her wait was not long. Dr. Wellington came in and sat.

"Ms. Belle."

"Doctor."

"I trust you've had a good day."

"I have, thank you. I was fitted for the ball gown; it's exquisite."

"Wonderful. And how did you sleep?"

"Well, to be honest, not very well at all."

"Oh? Why not?" Lucinda told him the same story she had told Ms. Poe of the previous night's events. He listened without reaction. A servant came into the room with their plates. She caught part of Lucinda's story and was so surprised; she dropped the plate. She couldn't believe this was being discussed. It had always been hush-hush in the house. Ms. Poe reprimanded them if they tried to speak of it.

Lucinda jumped when the plated hit the floor. She was obviously speaking of something taboo. The servant scrambled to the floor to clean up her mess. Dr. Wellington pushed his seat back and stooped down with the servant. He took her hands in his and said, "It's alright. Leave it."

"I'm so sorry, sir, it's just that—well...."

Dr. Wellington pulled her to her feet. "Really, it's alright. Go now, fetch another plate, and you can clean this up after we have finished."

"Yes, sir. Thank you, sir." She left and returned

moments later with a new plate of food. She looked at Lucinda in a puzzled way, still unable to believe what she had heard.

When Lucinda and Dr. Wellington were once again alone, he began his explanation with a story.

"Ms. Belle, it all began many, many years ago. The original owner of this home was also a physician—but of a monstrous sort. He was not in the profession to help others; he hurt many. He was a twisted man. He had hired help that would bring him lone travelers and vagrants—those who would not be missed. He performed terrible experiments upon them. They were kept alive for days, weeks, sometimes even months, while he experimented on them. When the poor souls finally died, he practiced necromancy on them. Have you heard the term before?"

"I have not. What does it mean?"

"It is raising the dead to do the necromancer's bidding."

"But that's not possible. Is it?"

"I can't say for sure. I can only say that there appear to be spirits trapped here in this house. We see them, hear them, and, at times, feel them. It is something we just don't discuss.

It seems to make the activity worse."

"I'm sorry. I didn't know. I won't speak of it again."

"It's not your fault. No one here has spoken of it for years, and your mere presence has caused a disturbance. I'm not sure why. I noticed it the first night you were here. I was following the specter when I found you down here. That is why I stress the importance of staying in your room—why I ask everyone to stay in their rooms with their doors locked. It doesn't go into the bedrooms; it stops short at the doors."

"I understand. I will be more mindful of keeping the door locked and staying in my room."

"Thank you. It is my desire for you and everyone else in the house to be safe. Now, enough of this discussion. I sent out the invitations today for the ball. I am looking forward to introducing you."

"Thank you. I am excited, but also a bit apprehensive. I have never been the center of attention before—only in the background serving a master, and a cruel one at that."

"You will be just fine. Enjoy yourself. Then, in a few weeks, you'll be off to etiquette school. Let's take dessert in the sitting room, shall we?"

They spent the rest of the evening in the sitting room discussing many issues. Dr. Wellington was amazed at Lucinda's knowledge and insight. He knew she would go far—she would do great things. They eventually retired for the night.

Chapter 5

The day of the ball had finally arrived. Lucinda had never seen such hustling and bustling and doting over her. She had always been the one working and preparing for such an event. This was an unusual experience for her—she was beginning to like it.

It was close to the time for guests to arrive, and Ms. Poe took Lucinda to wait in her room. Lucinda did as she was told; she sat and waited—waited in anticipation. Dr. Wellington wanted Lucinda to be presented to everyone in a grand manner. The closer it came to Lucinda's presentation, the more anxious she became.

Meanwhile, downstairs in the ballroom, Dr. Wellington greeted individual guests as they arrived. And each inquired about the mystery lady he was introducing that night. He simply said she was a very special person who stumbled into his life, and they would all meet her soon. No one knew that she had literally stumbled into his life.

When the last guest had arrived, Dr. Wellington sent a servant to fetch Lucinda. Ms. Poe accompanied Lucinda as she descended the stairs, and at the entrance of the ballroom, Lucinda was handed off to the good doctor. Everyone gasped at the sheer beauty of Lucinda Belle, and this pleased Dr.

Wellington.

However, there were a few guests who could scarcely believe what they were seeing—namely, Judge Whitman, his wife, and his daughter. The judge looked as if he were going to be ill. He had been certain Lucinda was homeless and desolate on the streets of Whitechapel, yet she stood here before him in the home of the richest and most distinguished man in London.

A servant handed Dr. Wellington a bell to acquire the attention of his guests. The ringing of the bell elicited complete silence. Dr. Wellington smiled at his guests as he took Lucinda by the arm and walked to the center of the room.

"Good evening, everyone. I would like to thank you all for attending tonight. I would like to introduce a most intriguing young lady, Lucinda Belle. I hope you all will embrace her into the community. She is destined for greatness. We can all benefit from knowing her. Now, shall we mingle and dance?" He gestured for the musicians to play.

The musicians played. The doctor's guests took turns introducing themselves to Lucinda. She met a duke and duchess, many lords and ladies, a baron and baroness, doctors, lawyers, politicians, and judges. Judge Whitman and his family did not introduce themselves to Lucinda.

So, when all other guests had greeted her, Dr. Wellington led Lucinda over to the Whitman family.

"Judge Whitman, I don't think you have greeted Ms. Belle tonight."

Judge Whitman was tongue-tied when he tried to speak. "Well—um, no, I haven't." His wife and daughter were equally astounded but at the same time extremely happy for Lucinda.

"Actually, doctor, this is my previous employer that I was telling you about. Don't you remember?" Lucinda said in an almost inaudible tone feeling a plethora of emotions ranging from anger to shame to sadness. She quickly pulled herself together and held her head high—she was no victim, she was strong.

"Ah, yes, I do remember," Dr. Wellington chimed in. "You said you left under strained circumstances. But we will be civilized and not go into that. We will let bygones be bygones and enjoy the night." Dr. Wellington smiled and took Lucinda by the arm, and led her to other guests to mingle.

Lucinda felt a great sense of justice knowing that Mrs.

Whitman, a relentless snoop, would not let it go until she had forced the judge to disclose the reason behind Lucinda's abrupt departure.

Lucinda made quite an impression on the other guests. Dr. Wellington wanted everyone to know she was special, intelligent, and capable. And he saw no reason to hide that she had previously been a servant. Dr. Wellington thought this would only cause undue gossip in the future.

The ball was a celebrated success. Everyone mingled, danced, laughed, and enjoyed themselves. Lucinda, growing tired and agitated long before the ball was over, went out into the gardens beneath a beautiful full moon. She was missing less than thirty minutes before Dr. Wellington realized she was no longer mingling with guests. He immediately set out to find her.

Mrs. Whitman noticed Dr. Wellington rush out. She also noticed that her husband and Lucinda were missing. She immediately had the urge to snoop, Dr. Wellington's words echoing in her ears. She found her way out of the ballroom and began to explore the house.

Dr. Wellington found Lucinda in the gardens. "Lucinda, where have you been? Why did you leave the ball?"

"I had to get out for a while. It was just so overwhelming."

"You will get accustomed to this type of thing soon enough. Now, shall we rejoin the others?" Dr. Wellington laced his arm through Lucinda's and they proceeded to head back to the ballroom but they didn't make it. Just after they entered the house, suddenly they heard a frightful, blood-curdling scream from a room in the back of the mansion.

As they headed in the direction of the scream, they encountered Judge Whitman coming from the library. "Judge, do you need something?"

"No I—I just needed a bit of air. It is very crowded tonight."

The three heard yet another scream, and then another. They ran toward the kitchen and bumped into Mrs. Whitman coming from the dining hall.

"What is all of the screaming?" Mrs. Whitman asked.

"We're not sure. We are headed that way now. It sounds like it's coming from the kitchen." Dr. Wellington kept walking as he answered her.

They entered the kitchen to find Ms. Poe in hysterics.

"She's dead! She's dead! Dr. Wellington, who could have done such a thing?" Ms. Poe staggered to her feet from the badly butchered body of a young woman. It was one of Dr. Wellington's guests, Emma Bronze, wife of Dr. James Bronze.

Her corpse was cut up worse than a butchered animal. The poor woman's stomach was split completely open to expose the yellow fat beneath the skin. Her skin was pulled back, and most of her organs were ripped out and scattered closely about the body. The rib bones were exposed, chipped from being hacked by a sharp knife. The corpse was drenched in blood. There was blood spattered all over the kitchen, and a butcher's knife lay in a pool of crimson beside the lifeless body. The scene was horrific. Even Doctor Wellington, accustomed to disturbing sights, was horrified.

Ms. Poe fell into Dr. Wellington's arms, sobbing uncontrollably. He held her close and asked her if she had seen or heard anything—how did she come to find the body? She just shook her head and said she had come in to check everything after the staff had cleaned up. He told her she should retire for the night, and he would talk to her in the morning.

"Doctor, may I help Ms. Poe to her room?" Lucinda

asked, as she took hold of Ms. Poe's arm to help steady her.

"Of course. Thank you." Lucinda helped Ms. Poe up to her room. By that time, the halls were teeming with curious guests. Dr. Wellington told his guests they must return to the ballroom, that he would make an announcement shortly. With the help of his staff, everyone was ushered back to the ballroom, where they anxiously awaited Dr. Wellington's announcement.

Dr. Wellington pulled his staff aside and ordered all but one to stay in the ballroom, to make sure none of the guests left. He called his best maid to the side. "Lila, you must get the coachman and you two must make haste into town to retrieve the inspector. Tell him there has been a ghastly murder here, and I have a house full of guests. Tell him he must come quickly. Now go!"

The maid did exactly as she was told.

Dr. Wellington went into the ballroom and explained to his guests what had happened. He assured them the inspector was already on his way. The ladies began to weep, the men tried to comfort. No one could believe it. Dr. Wellington stayed with his guests to insure that panic was kept at a minimum.

Lucinda stayed with Ms. Poe for a while. She helped her out of her clothes and into a nightgown. She helped her into bed. Finally, she said, "Ms. Poe, I must go to be with Dr. Wellington. He may need my assistance."

"You're right. I will be fine. You can go now."

Lucinda walked toward the door and Ms. Poe said, "Lucinda, thank you. You are a kind child."

Lucinda turned and smiled. "You're very welcome, Ms. Poe. I'm just returning the same kindness you have shown me." She returned to the ballroom, where she found Dr. Wellington talking with another doctor, Dr. Smyth; they were discussing the way the body had been butchered.

"Dr. Wellington, I don't mean to interrupt, but I thought you would want to know that Ms. Poe is in her bed and resting."

"Thank you, Lucinda."

Lucinda was surprised at the way Dr. Wellington had addressed her—not "Lucinda Belle" and not "Ms. Belle." She wondered what it meant, but she knew this was not the time to inquire or speculate.

Dr. Wellington took her by the hand and squeezed it

reassuringly. She returned the squeeze.

It wasn't long before the maid and the coachman returned with the inspector.

"Inspector Anderson, thank you so much for coming." Dr. Wellington said.

"You're very welcome, Dr. Wellington. Where is the body?"

"This way—to the kitchen." Dr. Wellington led the way. Lucinda and the inspector followed.

"Dr. Wellington, I have more men on their way. They should be here momentarily. Can you have one of your staff meet them when they arrive?"

"Of course." Dr. Wellington called out the young maid who had retrieved the inspector, "Lila, Inspector Anderson has more men on the way. Can you show the inspector's men to the kitchen when they arrive?"

"Yes, of course." She quickly went to the front door to wait on the other detectives.

When they reached the kitchen, the inspector had a horror-stricken look. He began to examine the scene. "When did you discover the body?

"Just before I sent, Lila, my servant girl, to fetch you."

Then there was a barrage of questions from the inspector—who found her, where was everyone, was there anyone unaccounted for, etc. Dr. Wellington, Lucinda, the staff, and Mr. and Mrs. Whitman were interviewed extensively, since they saw the body firsthand. Dr. Wellington would not let the inspector speak with Ms. Poe until the next day because she was so shaken. Then the inspector questioned all the guests.

After everyone had been questioned, they were allowed to leave. It was in the early hours of the morning before the house was completely cleared out. When all the guests had left, the inspector and his men took the body of Emma Bronze to the morgue. They would contact Dr. Bronze, who was out of town, that day, to inform him of his wife's gruesome and untimely death.

"Lucinda, I will see you to your room." Dr. Wellington offered.

"Actually, if you don't mind, I think I would like to sleep with Ms. Poe tonight. I think she needs company. She was very upset."

"Of course. That's very kind of you." Dr. Wellington

took Lucinda to Ms. Poe's room and unlocked the door. "Well, Lucinda, I am very sorry your ball ended in such a tragic way."

"Dr. Wellington, it's not your fault. I just feel so bad for the poor woman who was murdered."

"As do I. Well, goodnight."

"Goodnight, doctor." Dr. Wellington closed the door and locked it with his master key. He returned to his room and went to bed. He was so tired that, even in light of the evening's events, he fell sound asleep as soon as he lay down.

Lucinda took off her clothes, with difficulty, and borrowed one of Ms. Poe's nightgowns. She pulled the covers back and lay beside Ms. Poe.

Ms. Poe awakened as Lucinda tried to ease into the bed unsuccessfully trying not to disturb Ms. Poe. "Lucinda, what are you doing in here?"

"I'm sleeping here to watch over you. I don't think you should be alone tonight."

"Thank you. I think I will sleep better not being alone tonight." And she immediately fell back to sleep.

Lucinda was amazed at how well she herself slept that

night. She was fairly certain she had ever had such a restful sleep before.

Chapter 6

Lucinda awoke early. She went to the kitchen to prepare breakfast for Ms. Poe. She had almost forgotten about the mess in the kitchen from the night before. She had to step around the staff members cleaning blood from the floor and walls. Lucinda prepared Ms. Poe breakfast and took it up to her.

Lucinda set the tray with Ms. Poe's breakfast on the side table. "Ms. Poe," Lucinda said quietly.

Ms. Poe opened her eyes. "Good morning, Lucinda. What's this?" She looked at the tray of food.

"It's your breakfast. I thought you could use a little pampering this morning." Lucinda helped Ms. Poe sit up and placed the tray of food on Ms. Poe's lap.

"Did Dr. Wellington approve this special treatment?" Ms. Poe asked.

"No. I didn't ask him. I didn't think he would mind. He seems to be a kind and gentle master."

"He is. He shouldn't care this one time, under the circumstances." Ms. Poe ate her food. "Who made this?"

"I did. Is it not to your liking?"

"Oh, no. It's one of the best meals I have ever had. Thank you."

"I will go now. I understand the inspector will be back today. I should see if Dr. Wellington is up and stirring yet." Lucinda left, closing the door behind her.

Lucinda found Dr. Wellington in the gardens. He was terribly upset. "The inspector should be here soon. Is Ms. Poe awake?"

"Yes, she is having breakfast in bed."

"Breakfast in bed? How things have changed since your arrival. I assume breakfast in bed was your idea." He smiled wearily at Lucinda.

"Actually, yes. I thought she could use an act of kindness this morning."

"You provided an act of kindness last night. You felt the need to provide another today?"

"Yes, sir, I did." Lucinda answered defensively. She felt chastised by the doctor.

Dr. Wellington laughed. "Oh, Ms. Belle. That's good. Not only are you charitable, but you have the self-assurance to act without command nor permission. That's good—very good. You will go far."

"Well, Dr. Wellington, I only exhibit kindness to those who deserve it. And even though I was a servant for so many years, I do not like being commanded. I have the scars to prove it."

"As long as you are in my charge, you will never receive another scar." Dr. Wellington lightly stroked Lucinda's face with the back of his hand and smiled. "Will you retrieve Ms. Poe and ask her to prepare for Inspector Anderson? I would ask Lila or one of the other servants, but I think Ms. Poe considers you a friend, and she needs a friend now."

"I will be happy to fetch her. I hope she considers me a friend, as I consider her one. I have had very few of those in my life." Lucinda turned and went back to the house to fetch Ms. Poe.

Just as Ms. Poe and Lucinda descended the stairs, Lila answered a knock at the door; it was Inspector Anderson.

"Ms. Belle, Ms. Poe," the inspector greeted the women.

In unison they greeted him, "Inspector Anderson."

"Is Dr. Wellington home?" Lucinda was the only one who knew the whereabouts of Dr. Wellington, so she answered.

"Yes, inspector, he is in the gardens. Would you like me to fetch him?"

"Actually, it would probably be more private out there for our conversation."

"Very well. You can follow me."

"Ms. Poe, I will need to speak to you, as well. Can you come with us, please?"

"Of course, inspector." They went into the gardens together, where they found Dr. Wellington sitting on the bench where Lucinda had left him earlier.

"Dr. Wellington."

"Good morning, inspector. Come, have a seat. Hello, all. Ms. Poe."

Ms. Poe said in an almost inaudible voice, "Good morning, sir."

Inspector Anderson spoke. "Dr. Wellington, I really wish my visit was under better circumstances."

"So do I. I suppose you want to speak with Ms. Poe?"

"Yes." Lucinda stood up to walk away. She thought they would want privacy.

"Ms. Belle, you need not leave. If Dr. Wellington has no objections," Inspector Anderson said.

"Of course not. Ms. Belle has quickly become a very loved member of my strange family." Dr. Wellington smiled at her, making her face flush and her heart skip a beat.

"I don't want to intrude."

The doctor assured her she would be comforting to Ms. Poe during the questioning. Lucinda sat back down beside Ms. Poe.

The inspector questioned Ms. Poe about finding the body of Emma Bronze. Ms. Poe explained that she had gone back to the kitchen to check everything. This was something she did regularly, since she was ultimately responsible for every staff member, their actions, and their mistakes. She continued telling the inspector how she had stumbled upon the mangled corpse and immediately screamed. The next thing she knew, Dr. Wellington, Lucinda, and the Whitmans were there, and then other guests began to crowd the hallways to see what the screaming was about.

Lucinda hugged Ms. Poe, the woman seeming to fall

apart a little at a time as she told her story. It was obvious to the inspector that Ms. Poe had nothing to do with the murder. The inspector then dismissed Ms. Poe, but wanted to speak with Lucinda and Dr. Wellington again. Ms. Poe pleaded with the doctor to let her stay until they were finished. She didn't want to be alone. Both the doctor and the inspector agreed and allowed her to stay.

Lucinda recounted the events leading up to the gruesome scene, never loosening her hold on Ms. Poe. She needed to hold onto to Ms. Poe as much as Ms. Poe needed it.

When the inspector was satisfied with Lucinda, he turned his questioning to Dr. Wellington. The doctor explained how he had come to find Lucinda, the Whitmans, and then Ms. Poe and the corpse of Emma Bronze.

The inspector was satisfied with their stories. He thanked them for their time and left. Afterward, he proceeded to the Whitman home. The inspector felt everyone at the doctor's home was being honest with him. However, he had his suspicions about the Whitmans. He was anxious to question them once again.

After the inspector left, Lucinda took Ms. Poe to her room and stayed with her until she fell asleep. Then, she and the doctor spent a disconsolate and uneventful evening together. They tried not to think of or discuss the events of the previous night.

Inspector Anderson soon found himself at the Whitmans. He had been thinking in depth about everyone who might be a suspect, and the gruesome image of poor Emma Bronze's mangled body.

The inspector knocked on the door and one of Judge Whitman's servants answered.

"I'm Inspector Anderson. Are Judge and Mrs. Whitman home? They are expecting me."

"Judge Whitman is at his office. I believe Mrs. Whitman has stepped out, as well."

The inspector was not happy with this. The night before, they had agreed to meet with him to give a more in-depth statement. This made the inspector suspect the Whitmans were hiding something. Inspector Anderson told the servant to let the Whitmans know that he had come by. "Please tell them I was very disappointed they did not keep their appointment with me. I need them to come down to my office tomorrow—as soon as the station opens. If they do not show up, I will be forced to have them brought in for questioning." The inspector went back to his office to continue his investigation.

Chapter 7

The morning after the ball at Dr. Wellington's house, Judge Whitman decided not to meet with the inspector. The judge was appalled the police inspector would even entertain the thought of questioning him, a judge. Judge Whitman had instructed his wife to go out and ignore their appointment. They would meet with the inspector, but in the presence of their attorney.

Mrs. Whitman decided it was time to inquire about Lucinda. She had her suspicions about the reasons behind Lucinda's abrupt departure, especially after the comment Dr. Wellington made the night before. She was sure her husband, Isaiah, had something to do with Lucinda leaving.

"I will go out, and I will not meet with the inspector. However, I want you to tell me why Lucinda left."

The judge replied, "I told you I don't know why she left. Why are you bringing this up again?"

"I thought it was strange the way she left. But then, I saw the look on your face when you saw her last night. And when she told Dr. Wellington we were her previous employers, he made a comment about bygones being bygones. I know I never wronged her; she was my favorite.

And you looked afraid that she was going to say more."

There was total silence. The judge did not respond at all. Mrs. Whitman was beginning to regret her line of questioning. Judge Whitman's face distorted almost unrecognizably. Mrs. Whitman became very frightened. She didn't like confrontation with her husband because of his brutal and cruel nature, but her curiosity had to be satisfied.

The judge's rage grew instantly. "This is not up for discussion." He spoke the words through gritted teeth. "I do not answer to you! I am the man of the house—a judge, no less! You are lowly woman! You should know your place by now!" His voice grew louder and his body became more animated. He paced about the room, eventually knocking things from the fireplace mantle and the tables.

Mrs. Whitman had never seen him like this. He was a brutal man, and she herself would not have picked him for her husband. Her marriage was arranged by her parents and his. She knew that he, too, if given a choice in the matter, would have married another—the beautiful Emma Bronze. She was surprised by his lack of emotion when they had discovered the body. But even now, in the state the judge was in, Mrs. Whitman pressed him for a reason for Lucinda's departure. Judge Whitman continued to refuse her an answer.

One of the servants came to the room at hearing the commotion. She was fearful of what was happening to Mrs. Whitman. "I don't mean to interrupt, but I need Mrs. Whitman. I have some questions about the staff and duties."

"That's fine, take her from my sight before I do something we will both regret!" Judge Whitman barked.

Mrs. Whitman was disappointed by the interruption— she was determined to get an answer from her husband. But now, she had to deal with the running of the house.

"What is it? What couldn't wait?" she snapped at her faithful servant, Loraine.

"Just come with me, please." Once Loraine was sure they were out of earshot, she told Mrs. Whitman something important. "I heard two of the servants gossiping."

"Why should I care about servant gossip?"

"It was about Lucinda."

"What about Lucinda?" Mrs. Whitman asked.

"I know why she left. One of the servant girls saw your husband attack Lucinda. She struggled with him and was eventually able to fight him off. She then fled the house crying. No one knew what happened to her after that.

Knowing the judge's temper and what he was capable of, the servant was afraid to come forward. I overheard the gossip, and asked the servant what grounds she had to make such an accusation. She then told me she had seen the act first hand."

"Do you trust she is telling the truth?"

"I do. She needs this position. She would be homeless without it. She would never say anything to jeopardize it if it weren't true. I have never before caught her in an untruth. And besides, everyone here fears the wrath of the judge—including me."

"Thank you for telling me this. I knew there was more to Lucinda's disappearance. She is living with Dr. Wellington now. The ball last night was in her honor. If you had seen my husband's face when the doctor introduced her, you would have thought he saw a specter."

"Is that what the argument was about?"

"Yes. Thank you for sharing this information with me. Please tell any of the staff who may be privy to this not to mention it. I don't want the judge to know what we know. Besides, I can't be responsible for what he may do—with his temper and all."

"Yes, ma'am, I will make sure the staff share no further

gossip."

"Thank you. Now, I have something that I must do. Carry on as normal." Mrs. Whitman prepared herself to leave for the day and went to talk to her husband.

"Isaiah, I am leaving now. I want to leave before Inspector Anderson arrives. I wanted to apologize for my earlier actions. I know my position, and it is not to question the actions of my husband. There will be no further talk of Lucinda Belle."

"Thank you. I am leaving soon, as well. We don't want to give the inspector any further statements until I have met with Dawson."

Mrs. Whitman turned and left. She went directly into town. Mr. Daniel Dawson was the Whitmans's attorney. But Mrs. Whitman was on her way to see James Lawrence. He was an old friend who happened to be an attorney. He was the only person in the world Melinda Whitman could trust. She needed to confide in him, to tell him what she had discovered, and what had happened the night before at Dr. Wellington's ball.

Melinda Whitman stepped out of her carriage and into James Lawrence's office. He was surprised to see her. He stood immediately to greet her.

"Melinda, to what do I owe the pleasure? It is so nice to see you; it's been far too long. Come sit." He pulled a chair closer to his desk for her.

"Well, James, I think I may have some trouble with my husband."

"The good judge? That's not possible," James said sarcastically. He wasn't very fond of Judge Whitman. "What is it, Melinda?" It was obvious she was extremely distraught.

"I know men of power have many transgressions—that I learned long ago. But I just learned something about my husband, and I want to tell you something that happened last night."

"Melinda, whatever it is, you can tell me. You know I will help you in any way possible. What is troubling you?" James laid his hand upon Melinda's.

"I had a wonderful young servant who, a few weeks ago, just disappeared. She left without telling anyone. She took nothing of hers. Well, last night, I went to a ball at Dr. Wellington's for a young lady he has taken in. The woman ended up being my missing servant girl."

"How, pray tell, did she come to be with him?"

"I have no idea. But it gets stranger. When Dr. Wellington introduced us to her, Isaiah was noticeably shaken. He was obviously hiding something. And Dr. Wellington made a comment that I knew was directed at Isaiah, which made me even more suspicious. Later that evening, we all heard a scream and found Ms. Poe, one of Dr. Wellington's servants in the kitchen. She had discovered a dead body there. It was Emma Bronze." Melinda paused to take a breath and regain her composure; she was beginning to feel out of sorts.

"Emma Bronze was murdered? Melinda, what happened to Emma?"

"She was hacked to death."

"Do the police have any suspects?"

"I don't know. But that is another thing. Inspector Anderson arranged to come by for statements from my husband and myself this morning. I was ordered, by my husband, not to be there when the inspector came. My husband also left. He went to see Daniel Dawson."

"Why would he not want to give a statement? Why would he feel the need for an attorney?"

"Past indiscretions, I suppose. He and Emma were once lovers and she was found dead at a party he also attended. He was alone at the time of the murder. And, I was told today by my most trustworthy servant, the reason Ms. Belle left our service abruptly was because my husband attacked her. Afterward, she ran off."

"Does he know you are privy to this information?"

"No. You know what a brute he is. I did not want to face his cruelty.

"I see. It's best not to let him know what you know about Ms. Belle. Does he know you are aware of his past with Emma?"

"Yes, I confronted him when Emma confided in the wrong friend a year ago, and the gossip finally reached me."

"If he attacked this young servant girl, do you think that he has it in him to commit murder?"

"I think there is great potential for evil in that man. I am just so sorry for Lucinda, and relieved she is no longer in my house."

"Do you think Dr. Wellington knows what happened to Lucinda?"

"I feel sure. He was very rude and smug when he introduced her to Isaiah. It was as if to say, 'You can never hurt her again.' That was another thing piqued my suspicions."

"If you believe the judge was involved in the murder, maybe you should confide in Aleister Wellington. He is a man of many means and connections, and what's more, he has a kind and generous heart. He is a good person to have on your side. Meanwhile, I will speak to the inspector to see what I can get out of him about this murder."

"Thank you, James. I feel much better having confided in someone."

"Just keep your mouth shut, play dumb, and don't upset the judge. Please be cautious." He gave her a hug and sent her on her way, hoping this would not be the last time he saw her alive. He knew the judge could be very dangerous if provoked.

Mrs. Whitman did not want to make two suspicious trips away from home in one day—she did not want to alarm the judge. She shopped and visited old friends. Finally, when the sun was setting, she had her coachman drive her home, where Judge Whitman was waiting. He had stayed in his office all day, hiding from the inspector.

"Where have you been all day?" He commanded an answer.

"I went to several different friends' homes to visit. You told me not to be available for the inspector. I thought it best to stay away all day, in case he was persistent and came more than once."

"Well, it doesn't matter now. He has threatened to take us in if we don't come to his office willingly tomorrow morning. Besides, I talked to Daniel, and he said he thinks it's best to give our statements soon, while he accompanies us. Daniel and I have already planned to see the inspector in the morning. You must come with me. The inspector wants a statement from you. I don't know why, since you're a woman."

"I will be ready. Is there anything you want me to say— or not to say?"

"No, just tell him what you know, which I'm sure isn't much."

"Yes, dear."

They arrived early the next day at the inspector's office. Their attorney met them there, and was present as they gave their statements and answered the inspector's questions.

Then, Judge Whitman went to his office and his wife went back home.

Chapter 8

Days had passed since the inspector had come to the mansion. Lucinda felt very anxious. She often went to bed early. But, as before, she heard scratching outside her door. Delirious in her restless sleep, Lucinda let her mind wander. Did the thing in the night have some influence on the murder of Emma Bronze? She thought about it only for a moment. It was more of a passing thought than a real concern. Emma was dead, and there was nothing anyone could do about it.

But whatever it was haunting the house at night, it was not good. It felt evil, with malicious intent. She wondered if it was the previous owner, the doctor—the necromancer himself. Dr. Wellington must also have an uneasy feeling about it, otherwise he wouldn't insist on everyone barricading themselves in their rooms at night. Does he know more than he shared with her?

Not only was this thing frightening to Lucinda, but since she had been in the house, she had some unusual feelings she hadn't experienced since childhood. Her childhood was wrought with devastation and trauma, events she didn't like to talk or think about—things she had locked in a box in the depths of her subconscious. But after being in the doctor's house for only a few days, she began to remember things long forgotten.

At first, she thought they might be dreams, but as time passed, she realized they were memories from her childhood. As these memories increased, so did her anger. Even at the ball, when Lucinda's demeanor was silent and shy upon being introduced to the judge, inwardly she felt an intense anger. She wanted to yell at Dr. Wellington for inviting the man, and wanted to gouge out the judge's eyes—or worse, castrate him—for attacking her.

Lucinda always prided herself on her compassionate nature and kind heart, so these re-emerging emotions were beginning to frighten her as much as the thing outside her room. She felt as though she were coming apart at times. And after another sleepless night, she decided to speak to Dr. Wellington.

Dr. Wellington was already seated at the table in the dining hall when Lucinda arrived. "Good morning, Lucinda. You look lovely, as usual, though tired. Did you not sleep well again?"

"Actually, no. I heard something outside my room again last night. I didn't sleep well at all."

"I'm sorry. You only have a short while before you

depart for etiquette school, if you can just endure a little longer. I would do something about this if I could, but my hands are tied."

"I understand. I hardly expect you to control the spirit world. I just appreciate your generosity and kindness. But there is one thing I would like to discuss with you, if I may."

"Of course. You can speak to me about anything. What is it?" Dr. Wellington looked puzzled.

"Well, it is a childhood condition I thought I had overcome, but has resurfaced as of late," Lucinda began. She paused, biting her lower lip, regretting her decision to come forth.

"Yes. Continue." Dr. Wellington's curiosity was piqued.

"Well, as I told you before, my childhood was not a great one. Many things happened to me and my loved ones. By nature, I am a kind person, but as I endured tragedy after tragedy, I became angry. I had terrible thoughts about anyone whom I felt had wronged me. As I grew older, I was able to forget the bad things—much of my childhood. But I've found that, since I have been here, I have been remembering events hidden away in my head. The anger has resurfaced, also. I think it has something to do with the thing that paces outside my bedroom at night. I am becoming very frightened. I am afraid of losing control—losing myself. Can you help me?"

"I will try. But I think it has more to do with this house and its past than with you and your past."

"What do you mean? Is there more to the story of the necromancer?"

"Lucinda, I wasn't completely honest with you before. But I feel certain he opened a door to Hell itself. I believe this house has become a portal for evil to come and go as it pleases. And I think you have somehow stirred things up in this house. As I mentioned earlier for years, there had been activity, but not this much. One of the staff or myself would hear or see something, maybe once or twice a month. But since you have been staying here, things seem to happen daily. It was something we never spoke of, but now, with so much activity, we can no longer ignore it."

"Do you think evil is trying to gain control over me?"

"I think it will be best to get you and keep you away from this house soon."

"There is something else," Lucinda said. "At times, I find myself thinking of Mrs. Bronze. Do you think the evil in this house had something to do with her demise? I have been feeling so angry lately, I'm afraid I may not know what I am capable of. Do you think it could have been me?"

"Of course not. No matter how angry you become, you are not capable of such a gruesome, evil act. And besides, even if you were, what motive would you have?"

"I suppose you're right. I just feel confused."

"You will be leaving this place soon. And you will be back to your old self after that." Dr. Wellington assured her.

"But when I leave, if I should not come back here, will I never see you again?"

"Of course not. There is no way I would allow that. I will be coming to Lady's Kingston's to visit often. And I will send for you to travel with me on occasion."

"That's good," Lucinda said in a small voice.

"Let's take a walk, shall we? I think you need some fresh air." Dr. Wellington led Lucinda to the stables. "I think we should ride. Can you ride, Lucinda?"

"Yes."

"Good. I have something I think you shall enjoy."

"A present? You really need not. You have done so much already."

"A small gift, that's all."

When they arrived at the stables a few minutes later, the stable boy brought a beautiful black mare to Lucinda and handed her the reigns. It was the same horse she had admired the first day she had gone to the stables with Dr. Wellington, Lady Jane. The horse was already saddled and ready to ride. Lucinda gasped. She couldn't believe the doctor was allowing her to ride his prize mare.

"Oh, Dr. Wellington, I can't ride her. She is your prize mare." Lucinda shook her head.

"Oh, she is my favorite. But she no longer belongs to me. She's a gift to you." Dr. Wellington smiled.

"Oh, no. I can't accept her."

"Please. She really likes you, and you love her, I can tell. I know you will be good together. She will be going with you to the etiquette school."

"They allow students to bring horses?"

"No, but I have made a substantial contribution to the school, and as a favor you will be allowed to have her with

89

you. You will need a companion."

"I do so love her. She is quite beautiful. Are you sure about this?"

"I am. Will you please accept?"

"I shall. Thank you so much. And it will be great to have her with me, since I won't have you or Ms. Poe."

"Shall we ride?"

Lucinda was happy. All the old memories and angry urges completely disappeared. She had fallen in love with Lady Jane at first sight, and now the beautiful mare belonged to Lucinda.

Dr. Wellington and Lucinda rode the horses for hours. Then, they stopped in a meadow under some willow trees by a sparkling brook.

"Are we watering the horses?" Lucinda asked.

"Yes, and something more." Dr. Wellington dismounted his stallion and took a satchel from behind his saddle.

"What do you have there?" Lucinda dismounted Lady Jane and stepped to the side to see what he had.

"I thought it would be nice for us to have lunch outside today." Dr. Wellington took from the satchel a blanket, some fruit, cheese, pork, bread, and a bottle of wine. He spread the blanket on the ground beside the brook. He then placed the food on the blanket. The horses grazed in the meadow and drank from the brook while Dr. Wellington and Lucinda had lunch.

Lucinda had never in her wildest dreams thought this life was possible. She was dazzled by her treatment by Dr. Wellington. The minute she met him, she knew he was a good and kind man, though at first she couldn't help but be a bit suspicious of his motives for taking her in—she had become distrusting because of her past. Lucinda also thought he was very attractive. The more familiar he became, the more attractive he was, until she finally realized she had fallen in love with the good doctor.

"Dr. Wellington, this is such a treat. You are too kind to me. Thank you so much."

"Lucinda, we have become very close. I think it's time you call me Aleister."

"But that is too intimate. What will people say—what will they think?"

"Does it really matter? And besides, it is no one's business what our relationship is."

"And just what is our relationship? I am not yet clear on that."

"I think it is obvious I have feelings for you. I have never tried to keep that a secret. I just did not want to pursue you before you were comfortable, especially after what you have been through."

"So, just what are you trying to say Dr.—um, Aleister."

"I would like to formally court you, if you would allow it." Lucinda became so excited she lost her breath. All of a sudden, her corset felt much too tight restricting her breath. "Aleister, I feel like I may faint. I can't breathe."

Dr. Wellington immediately went to unbutton Lucinda's dress to loosen her corset and help her breathe. Instinct made Lucinda jump away, not sure of what he was about to do.

"Lucinda! Hold still. You will faint if we don't loosen that corset. I think Ms. Poe may have laced it a bit too tight this morning." He pulled her back down to the blanket. When she came to her senses, she stopped resisting.

Dr. Wellington quickly unbuttoned her top and pulled it away hastily. This only made Lucinda's heart quicken, and her breathing grew more intense from the uneasiness of him undressing her. He quickly untied the corset. As soon as the corset was loosened, Lucinda got her breath.

"Is that better?" Dr. Wellington asked.

"Much. Thank you," Lucinda answered, taking in deep breathes.

"Well?"

"'Well,' what?" Lucinda looked puzzled. She had gotten so anxious over the question, and then at having the doctor half undress her, that she forgot the question altogether.

"May I court you?"

"Well, yes, of course. I would like that very much."

Dr. Wellington was so excited, he reacted without thinking. He leaned in and kissed her passionately. Lucinda once again found herself struggling to breathe. For a moment, her mind flashed to the last man who had touched her this way. But this was different somehow. She returned the kiss with just as much passion. Dr. Wellington did something very much out of character; he began to strip away the rest of Lucinda's clothes. She did something out of character as well by letting him. Passion filled them both, and in a matter of minutes they were both naked in the beautiful meadow, amongst the animals. Lucinda likened it to the Garden of Eden—they were about to have a bite of forbidden fruit. And she wanted it.

Aleister kissed Lucinda deeply. Lucinda gasped and her brain raced between panic and pleasure, fear and felicity. She accepted him with desire. It was a hunger they both felt; they knew this was the only way to satiate it. It was pure ecstasy—a euphoria that could compare to nothing else in the world.

After they had finished, they dressed themselves. However, Lucinda, even with the doctor's help, could not get her clothes to look the way Ms. Poe had. When Ms. Poe helped her undress later, she would know something was amiss. Lucinda wondered if she should tell Ms. Poe what had happened, or make up a story.

"Lucinda, I hope I did not pressure you into this. Was this what you wanted?"

"Of course it was. If you know one thing about me, it is that I am defiant. You would have known if I objected. Was it what you wanted?" Lucinda asked, suddenly shy.

"Yes. I have wanted nothing in the world more since I met you. As I grew to know you and spent more time with you, I found it harder to control myself. To be clear, though, I did not plan this. I'd just planned to have a nice lunch and distract you from the house. You do believe me, don't you?"

"Yes, Aleister, I believe you. And to be honest, each day I found it harder to be with you, thinking you were only my benefactor. I wanted more from you. I wanted this. Thank you for a wonderful day."

Dr. Wellington held Lucinda for the longest time before he pulled away. "We really should be getting back."

"I know."

They packed everything up and raced their horses back to the stables, where the stable boy, Miles, was waiting to take the horses upon their return. They left the horses in his care and returned to the house. Upon approaching the house, an ominous feeling came over Lucinda. It was a darkness in her heart.

When they entered the house, they were surprised to hear that Melinda Whitman was waiting for them. Ms. Poe greeted the pair as they entered the house.

"Mrs. Whitman is here. She has been here for hours

waiting. She insisted that she must speak to you, and it must be today. I hope you don't mind that I let her wait."

"Of course not, Ms. Poe. I trust your judgment. Where is she?"

"She is in the parlor."

"I will find something to occupy my time during your meeting." Lucinda turned to walk away.

"Ms. Belle, she wants to speak with you both. You must meet with her, as well." Ms. Poe lightly took Lucinda's elbow to halt her from leaving.

Lucinda looked at Dr. Wellington, puzzled. "Should I come with you?"

"Mrs. Whitman wants to speak with us both." He put out his arm for Lucinda to take. "Shall we go?" Dr. Wellington thanked Ms. Poe and dismissed her. He and Lucinda walked into the parlor, arm in arm.

"Mrs. Whitman, to what do I owe the pleasure? And what of Judge Whitman?" Dr. Wellington and Lucinda sat on a couch together across from Melinda Whitman.

"To be honest, Dr. Wellington, my husband is unaware of my visit today. He would be very upset if he knew. I was hoping we could keep this confidential." Melinda was obviously very upset.

"Of course. To be honest, I am not very fond of your husband," Dr. Wellington said.

"You and me both. And I'm sure Lucinda can join that consensus."

"Yes, indeed." Dr. Wellington's demeanor instantly changed and became harsh. It was at that moment that Melinda Whitman knew the servant's story about her husband was regretfully true. She also suspected there was more to the doctor and Lucinda's relationship than was being disclosed. "I have come to ask for your help, doctor, and for Lucinda's forgiveness."

"I would be happy to help, but as far as Lucinda is concerned, that's between you and her."

"First, I will address Lucinda, and as my story progresses, what I am asking of you will become clear." Melinda Whitman turned to Lucinda and, with tears in her eyes, she spoke. "Lucinda, I have recently come to discover why you left my service. I would like to apologize to you for not being there, and for failing to protect you. You were always my favorite servant, and I loved you like my own daughter. I was devastated when you left. Had I known, I would have surely done something."

"Mrs. Whitman, I place no blame on you for your husband's actions. I know you have no control over him. You could not have done anything to protect me, short of endangering your very life. I did not tell you why I left because I just had to get away from the judge. How did you come to find out?"

"One of my servants told me. She overheard two other servants gossiping. Isaiah does not know I have found out. I don't want him to know. He is such a cruel creature, he would make sure I paid for merely holding the knowledge of his deeds." Mrs. Whitman's eyes filled with tears.

"Don't worry. Nothing will ever be said about this." Lucinda stood and walked over to Melinda Whitman. She knelt beside the weeping woman and hugged her. "I always loved you as a mother." Lucinda stood and went back to her seat beside Dr. Wellington.

Still weeping, Mrs. Whitman turned to Dr. Wellington. "This brings me to why I need your help. You should know that Isaiah had a love affair with Emma Bronze about a year ago. She couldn't be discreet, and the gossip found its way back to me. I confronted him and he was furious, but he confessed. I knew my husband was a cruel brute then, but I never dreamed he was evil enough to do what he did to Lucinda. Now, I have reason to suspect him of worse."

"Are you saying you think the judge could be responsible for Emma's murder?" Dr. Wellington asked.

"I didn't think so until recently. He was alone at the time of the murder."

"Mrs. Whitman, let me play devil's advocate for a moment. You knew of his affair and you, too, were alone and unaccounted for during the time of the murder. You had a motive; this was a woman who slept with your husband." Dr. Wellington said.

"Had I murdered Emma, that would make it an act of jealousy, correct?"

"Yes." Dr. Wellington agreed.

"In order to exhibit jealousy, one must posses the emotion of love, correct?"

"Well, yes. Of course."

"Then that theory should exonerate me. You see, doctor, I do not love my husband. In fact, if I had murdered someone that night it would have been him, not Emma."

"I understand."

"I have discussed this with James Lawrence. He suggested I come to you for help. He thought you should be aware of what I know. He is looking into it at the police station with the inspector. He is keeping my secret as well."

"Would you and your daughter like refuge here?" asked Dr. Wellington. "I don't think that's necessary just yet."

"What is it you ask of me, then?"

"I want you to protect Lucinda. I also want you to seriously consider my husband as a suspect. Have someone other than the police investigate him. He has many ties in the police department, you have to know that."

"Of course, I will get on it right away. And, as far as taking care of Lucinda, that is my utmost priority."

"I know. It's obvious. She is very lucky to have you. When will you make it public?"

"Excuse me?" Dr. Wellington asked, shocked.

"Oh, don't be coy. Any blind man can see that you love her, and she loves you."

Dr. Wellington blushed. "To be honest, I just asked to

court her this morning on our ride."

"That's wonderful. Do me a favor, would you?" Mrs. Whitman asked.

"Yes, of course." Dr. Wellington couldn't imagine what she wanted.

"When you announce it officially, make sure my husband and I are there. I want to see the look on his face."

Dr. Wellington smiled. "As you wish. But please, promise you will come here if you feel unsafe. It doesn't matter what time of night or day."

"I will. And thank you, Lucinda, for your forgiveness." Lucinda and Melinda Whitman hugged one another. Dr. Wellington kissed the back of Mrs. Whitman's hand and they bid each other farewell. Melinda stepped into her carriage and headed back to her home. She finally had a sense of relief.

Lucinda and Aleister were surprised by the revelation from Melinda Whitman. It seemed the judge would be a main suspect in the murder if Inspector Anderson were aware of Judge Whitman's relationship with Emma. Lucinda and Dr. Wellington spoke briefly about Mrs. Whitman's visit. They had their evening meal and went to bed early. They were both tired from their day of riding and lovemaking by the brook.

Lucinda had only been asleep a few hours when she heard something beyond her door. She didn't even stir. She had become accustomed to the pacing. It only took a few minutes for her to fall back into a deep sleep—a sleep that would render terrible nightmares.

Lucinda dreamed she was Emma Bronze being hacked to death. Then she dreamed she was another woman—a prostitute who met a similar fate as Emma. Suddenly, she was no longer the victim in her dream, but the murderer. She gained great pleasure from torturing and killing her victims. After all, they deserved it—they were whores. Emma was no better than the prostitute in the back alleys. In the dream, Lucinda felt as though this was justice for their crimes.

Lucinda awoke with a start. She was wet with sweat. She was horrified at the dream, and even more at the emotions she experienced in the dream. Lucinda feared she was becoming a monster because of the evil in the house. Was the house influencing her thoughts and emotions? Could she be capable of such an atrocity?

Lucinda tried to sleep, but the dreams kept recurring. They were not exactly the same, but similar in nature. Lucinda found herself wondering if she had indeed murdered Emma Bronze and had blocked it out. Finally, Lucinda could sleep no more. She got up and, against the doctor's wishes, left her room and roamed the house in the night.

When Lucinda reached the parlor, she sat in the dark. As she sat, she heard footsteps again. Something was different. This time she did not fear it. She did not want it to leave. Instead she wanted to know it—know what it was, why it was.

She called out in the dark. "Who are you? What do you want of me?" She sat quietly, awaiting a response, but heard nothing—only the continuation of approaching footsteps. When the footsteps stopped, even in the pitch black of the house, she knew the being was standing before her. "I can feel your presence. I know you are there. What do you want? What are you?"

Then she felt something cold brush against her arm. It left an ominous, sad feeling in her heart. Lucinda also felt rage and anger, she felt depressed and enthralled at the same time. She experienced a plethora of emotions—most were negative. But she derived pleasure from the negative feelings. She was so confused. She sat there the remainder of the night, in the dark, feeling this string of emotions. She was almost in a state of shock when Dr. Wellington came down and found her there the next morning.

"Lucinda, it is still dark out. Why are you just sitting here? What has happened to you?"

Lucinda looked up slowly and with cold black eyes that made Dr. Wellington tremble in fear, said, "It made contact with me. I know it now. I felt its evil. It was sent here from Hell to wreak havoc on men. It will succeed if it gets out of this house—if it hasn't already." Lucinda blinked her eyes a few times, and they were beautiful emerald green once again.

The doctor thought she must have been possessed. "Lucinda, are you alright?"

"I'm fine now. I think. I just felt so many negative emotions throughout the night. It touched me, and I knew it was evil. I felt the hatred it had toward men. I was very frightened. Aleister, can we leave this place and stay somewhere together until I go to Lady Kingston's?"

"Yes, of course. We must get you out of here as soon as possible. I have a cottage up north in the forest. It is very secluded. We can leave immediately. Pack your things."

"Can Ms. Poe come? I don't want to leave her here."

"Of course."

The three packed their bags and left that morning.

Chapter 9

Lucinda and Dr. Wellington enjoyed their time in seclusion together. They had small informal meals, walked around the property, they read, and they talked. It was nice not to have the hustle and bustle of social life for a change.

Ms. Poe enjoyed the relaxation as well, not having to run a huge house. She felt relieved only having to care for two people and a small cottage—no elaborate meals, no parties, and no guests. All three enjoyed not having to barricade themselves in their rooms at night.

Lucinda had calmed down somewhat. Only in a matter of hours of being on the property, her anger and anxiousness had subsided. However, at times she still felt the emotions arise.

Time passed quickly for them all—soon, two weeks had passed and it was time for Lucinda to go to Lady Kingston's, and for Dr. Wellington and Ms. Poe to return to the mansion. Dr. Wellington and Ms. Poe accompanied Lucinda to Lady Kingston's Etiquette School.

Lucinda's things had already been delivered by Dr. Wellington's staff, and the coachman brought Lady Jane. When Lucinda and the others arrived on campus, they were greeted by the headmistress, Sylvia Dalton.

"Dr. Wellington, what a pleasure. I was thrilled to hear you were sending me someone you regard so highly." She turned and smiled at Lucinda. Lucinda felt herself blush when she heard someone else talk about how much Dr. Wellington thought of her.

"Lucinda, I believe you will be very happy here," Ms. Dalton continued. "I know it will be an adjustment. I understand you have become very close to Dr. Wellington and Ms. Poe, but you need not worry. There will be time for you to visit them, and they will be able to come here. And Lucinda, you will find people here you will come to regard as family."

"I'm sure I will enjoy my time and benefit greatly from my experience here. Thank you for allowing me a spot. I will not disappoint you." Lucinda curtseyed.

"Ms. Belle has shown great potential, and she is a very knowledgeable young woman. I think she will do well here. Also, she has an acquaintance who attends here. Ms. Dalton, has Victoria Whitman arrived yet?" Dr. Wellington asked politely.

"Actually, yes. She arrived early this morning. Victoria

is in her room unpacking. I believe the Whitmans are still here, as well. Shall we get Lucinda settled in?"

"Yes, thank you." Dr. Wellington said.

Ms. Poe helped Lucinda put her things away and get her room in order. It seemed like they had been in Lucinda's room forever. Lucinda wanted to spend as much time with Dr. Wellington as possible before he left. Lucinda and Ms. Poe finally finished all of Lucinda's preparations, and they returned downstairs to look for Dr. Wellington and Ms. Dalton. On the way, they bumped into Victoria.

Victoria hugged Lucinda, and Lucinda returned the hug. The two girls were very close when Lucinda was in service of the Whitmans. Victoria never looked down on Lucinda because she was a servant. She felt more like Lucinda was a sister.

Victoria was so excited and inquired about many things at once. "Oh, Lucinda, you look lovely. It is so good to see you. I understand you will be attending Lady Kingston's this year, right? I think our rooms are side by side. Have you seen my mother yet?"

Lucinda tried to answer all of Victoria's questions. "I am attending Lady Kingston's. I have not seen your mother yet. I am very pleased our rooms are close. I am very happy you are here. I think that it will make it easier for me to adjust. I am still having problems fitting into this new world."

"Don't worry, I will help you. Let's go find my mother."

"Actually, I was hoping to find Dr. Wellington and spend a while with him before he left."

"Ah, of course. I saw him in the gardens with Ms. Dalton. I think I overheard a conversation about Lady Jane, whoever that is."

Lucinda giggled. "Lady Jane is my horse. I was allowed to have her here to help me adjust."

"Oh, my. Not many are granted such privileges. And you have a horse?"

"Yes, it was a gift from Dr. Wellington."

"Well, Lucinda, it seems like he is smitten on you."

"I wouldn't say that." Lucinda smiled coyly.

Ms. Poe pulled at Lucinda's arm. "Ms. Belle, we should really find Dr. Wellington." She didn't want Lucinda to be coaxed into divulging too much about her relationship with

Dr. Wellington, too soon.

"Of course." Lucinda agreed.

"Well, I should find mother before she leaves. I will see you soon." Victoria flitted off like a sprite. Lucinda envied Victoria's lightheartedness and freedom.

Lucinda and Ms. Poe went to the garden where they found Dr. Wellington and Ms. Dalton.

"Ah, Ms. Belle, are you all settled in?" Dr. Wellington took Lucinda's hand. He squeezed it tightly.

Lucinda felt his love radiate throughout her body. She smiled and bowed her head shyly, amazed at his boldness in front of the headmistress. "Yes, Dr. Wellington. Thank you."

"Ms. Dalton, there is something I would like you to be aware of before I leave. Ms. Belle—Lucinda—is not only my charge. I have asked to court her and she has given me permission. I hope in the near future to take her as my wife."

Lucinda could not believe what she was hearing. He had not mentioned that he would be telling the headmistress. Lucinda's knees buckled and she nearly fell. He caught her.

Ms. Dalton snickered behind her fan. "Dr. Wellington, maybe you should have informed Ms. Belle before divulging such intentions to me."

"Obviously. But with as much time as we have spent together the past few weeks, I thought she knew my intentions."

"Well—no! How would I have had any idea, Aleister? I cannot read minds," Lucinda blurted out. Then she collected herself. "I'm sorry. Forgive me, Dr. Wellington, Ms. Dalton. That is obviously not acceptable behavior for a lady."

Ms. Poe hid a smile behind her hand. She was thrilled Dr. Wellington had met his match. This woman would challenge him and make him happy.

"Lucinda, we are all friends here. Sylvia is the headmistress, but she is also my cousin. My adoptive father's niece. We have been as close as siblings most of our lives. Sylvia came to spend summers and Christmases with us. She is well aware of our relationship."

Lucinda did not like being in the dark. "Well, then, Aleister, thank you so much for sharing this with me," Lucinda replied angrily. She gritted her teeth and pulled her arm away.

Dr. Wellington glanced at Ms. Poe and Ms. Dalton, wishing this conversation could be in private. "Lucinda, I wasn't trying to hide anything from you. It's just that we have had so much going on with the murder, the house, and the move. Our relationship was progressing so fast. I didn't want to waste time discussing the school; I knew you were dreading it."

"Then why are you making me stay?" Lucinda took his arm back and began to cry.

"Ms. Poe, will you walk with me and tell me of any special needs that Lucinda may require?" Ms. Dalton said quickly, noticing the need for privacy.

"Of course, Ms. Dalton."

After the women left them, Dr. Wellington took Lucinda in his arms and held her closely. "Lucinda, I really don't want to be away from you, but you know how I feel about the house. Even before I fell in love with you, I knew you had to leave that house. Besides, you need to be acquainted with the most influential socialites in England if you plan on becoming my wife."

"Are you formally asking for my hand?"

"Yes, I guess I am. Will you be my wife, Lucinda Belle?"

Lucinda smiled like never before. "Yes. Yes, I will." She put her arms around his neck and squeezed until he thought he would suffocate.

"Shall we keep it private for a while?" Lucinda hoped the answer would be "no."

"Perhaps for a while. But not long, I promise."

Ms. Dalton and Ms. Poe returned. They were laughing and sharing a private joke. "If you two lovers are finished with your spat; dinner is served. Will you join us, Aleister?"

"I would be honored, cousin." He took Lucinda on one arm and Sylvia on the other as they went to the dining hall. Ms. Poe made her way to the kitchen to dine with the servants.

Dr. Wellington had a proud look on his face when he came into the dining hall and saw Judge Whitman. He knew then what he must do. When everyone had been seated, he picked up his water glass and clanked the side of it with his spoon.

"Ladies and gentlemen, I know this is an informal place to do this, but I must. This is something I am compelled to announce. Earlier this afternoon in the gardens, Ms. Lucinda Belle agreed to become my wife."

At least this time, Lucinda was sitting. She was once again surprised by the doctor's actions, but at the same time, thrilled. Sylvia Dalton smiled as she looked around at the expressions on everyone's faces. Melinda Whitman hid a slight smile from her husband. Victoria was beaming with excitement. Judge Whitman looked like he had been kicked in the groin—red in the face, bulging veins on his neck. Several other people gasped or whispered.

"No doubt this will be the talk of London—a doctor taking a servant girl to be his wife. That's fine; feel free to speculate and gossip. But Lucinda Belle is royalty in my eyes, and I am deeply in love with her. That is it." Dr. Wellington put down his glass, turned to Lucinda, and kissed her on the mouth, right at the dinner table.

The younger women in the room giggled. Most everyone seemed excited about the news of their new school mate. Poor Mrs. Whitman couldn't show her happiness, but Lucinda could tell she was indeed happy. Judge Whitman looked down at his plate and did not speak throughout the entire meal.

After the meal, Dr. Wellington and Lucinda spent a few precious moments together before he departed. They were both distraught by the idea of his departure. But it was for the best. Ms. Poe met Dr. Wellington at the carriage, where she bid Lucinda a tearful goodbye. It broke Lucinda's heart; she had grown to care for Ms. Poe. Then, Ms. Dalton and Victoria escorted Lucinda to her room.

Ms. Dalton bid the girls goodnight and retired to her own room. Victoria stayed and visited with Lucinda; she had to know all about Dr. Wellington and how they came to be betrothed. Lucinda did not share the details behind the reason she left the Whitman home, but she told Victoria nearly everything else. Victoria gazed into space, imagining every little detail.

After the girls had spent several hours talking, Victoria asked if she could stay for Lucinda's first night there. Lucinda appreciated her friendship with Victoria. She dreaded spending the night alone in yet another strange house. It would be wonderful to have a friend there, in case she became anxious or upset. She might sleep better.

"Thank you, Victoria, that would be wonderful. Would Ms. Dalton mind?"

"No. And if she did, I don't think she would say anything to you. Well, then, I will go to my room and get changed. I will be back soon." Victoria flitted away like some mythical creature.

Lucinda changed into her nightgown. It was odd not having Ms. Poe to help her, which was ironic since Ms. Poe's assistance was fairly recent for Lucinda to have become so accustomed to it. Lucinda was deep in thought, daydreaming about Aleister. She couldn't believe he had asked her to marry him and, not only that, but had actually announced their engagement to everyone at dinner. She smiled when she thought of how the announcement had upset the judge.

Victoria returned and noticed the smile on Lucinda's face. "Lucinda Belle, you look positively chuffed! Are you thinking about a particular handsome doctor?"

"Yes, actually, I was. I miss him already. I think this is going to be very hard. And I don't even know how long I have to stay here."

"You will stay until you finish your curriculum. But you have an advantage they are unaware of. Remember all the times we studied together? When I was puzzled, you helped me. You are very smart. So etiquette school should be a breeze for you."

"I don't know about that. Your dear mother was a good tutor." Lucinda said.

"This is true. It is funny my father never knew how

much my mother taught us both."

"That's good. Had he found out, we would have all received a thrashing."

They laughed together. Lucinda felt like everything would be fine. She just had to wait a little while. She would soon be Lucinda Wellington, wife of Dr. Aleister Wellington, and no longer Lucinda Belle the servant girl.

The two girls went to bed and slept well. Lucinda could barely believe it. She slept so well, in fact, when she awoke to the cock's crow, she momentarily forgot where she was. She expected to see Dr. Wellington at the breakfast table. Then she turned and saw Victoria lying beside her, realized where she was, and her heart sank.

Victoria awoke to Lucinda, rustling about, trying to find the dress she had decided to wear that day. "Lucinda, you are no longer a servant. You no longer have to wake at the crack of dawn. We ladies do get to sleep in a little later than the rooster." Victoria giggled.

Lucinda smiled. "I know, I just wanted to visit Lady Jane before breakfast. She makes me feel connected to Aleister—like I have a small piece of him still with me."

"Shall I accompany you to the stables?" Victoria rolled

over and stretched.

"That is not necessary. You go back to sleep and sleep in like a lady," Lucinda smiled. Victoria rolled back over and closed her eyes.

Lucinda dressed and went directly to the stables. It was barely light out. Dew covered the ground and the air was moist. It felt good to Lucinda—brisk and refreshing. She opened the door to the stables to find Lady Jane, also ready to face the day. Lucinda found the oats and scooped some out. Lucinda hung around Lady Jane's neck, closed her eyes, and breathed deeply. It was such a satisfying feeling. Suddenly, Lucinda jumped with a start when someone touched her. It was one of the stable hand, Roy.

He gruffly growled through clenched teeth, "What are you doing here? No one is supposed to be down here without permission. I wasn't told anyone would be here."

"I—well, Lady Jane is my horse. I came to see her before breakfast. I wasn't aware I needed permission to visit my own horse," Lucinda stammered.

"That's impossible. I have been a hand here for years, and Dalton has never approved such a thing. You're lying, and I don't care why. You socialites think you can do whatever you please. Just get out!"

Lucinda became furious. Not only was she being reprimanded for visiting her own horse, but she was being called a liar. "Sir, I will have you know that I am no liar!"

Roy grabbed Lucinda by both arms and squeezed, causing extreme pain. He was losing control. He hated the fact that these women had such liberties and he was put in the position to be their hired hand. "I don't care who you are or how much money you have, you are in my stables and you will do as I say. Who knows you're down here?"

Lucinda panicked. She recognized the look in the stable hand's eyes. She had seen it in another man's—Judge Whitman. Lucinda began to panic and she suddenly regretted her decision to visit her horse. "My friend knows. She is probably wondering why I am not back to my room yet. I should go. So, if you'll please release me, sir, I will be on my way and trouble you no further."

"I don't think so. You have already troubled me, and I think you should stay a bit longer. You didn't want to leave when I told you to, so now you will stay until I say you can go."

The man pulled at her bodice. Lucinda struggled and

freed one hand, slapping him hard. In turn, he struck her in the face, causing her lip to bleed. He grabbed a rope hanging on a nearby hook and tied her hands together. "This should hold you," he said, as he grappled with her dress tail. He became frustrated with Lucinda's constant struggle, so he put his hands around her throat and squeezed.

Lucinda could see the early morning light fade into black. She knew she was dying, and all she could do was think about her beautiful Aleister and the life they were to be denied. Then, her vision went completely black.

Suddenly, someone unseen struck Roy in the back of the head with a large piece of wood. Roy fell to the ground as he was struck in the face and head over and over, blood spattering the stalls. With each blow, pieces of flesh were chunked away by the rough bark of the stick. His skull cracked under the force of the blows. Then the unseen attacker began savagely assaulting the body. Roy was brutally beaten to death. His face was crushed beyond recognition. His body had received such horrific blows that his torso had burst open, spilling his internal organs onto the ground.

Lucinda, her hands still tied, lay motionless beside him.

Later that morning, Victoria came to breakfast and asked Headmistress Dalton if Lucinda had returned from the stables. Ms. Dalton was surprised at the question—she had no idea Lucinda was out of the building so early in the morning. The two questioned several girls, and no one had seen Lucinda, so they made haste to the stables.

There Lucinda lay, bloody, in ripped clothing, and unconscious. Just in front of her lay the battered, unrecognizable body of the stable hand, Roy. Victoria screamed, and soon others from the school began to arrive to see what had happened. Ms. Dalton stepped over the battered corpse of the man, fearing that Lucinda was already dead. To her surprise, when she began to untie Lucinda's hands, she stirred.

"Lucinda? Oh, Lucinda, I thought surely you were dead." Ms. Dalton was relieved to discover Lucinda was still alive.

Victoria could not stop screaming. Finally, some of the school's staff made their way to the stables. Ms. Dalton instructed them to get the other girls back to the school and send for the school doctor. She had the gardener carry Lucinda back to her room to be treated.

Once Lucinda was safe and settled into her bed, Ms. Dalton called for one of the senior staff members, a governess named Mary Roberts, to go into town and fetch one of the inspectors right away. She also penned a quick note to Dr. Wellington for Mary to deliver on her way back from town. Ms. Dalton locked down the school and forbade anyone to leave their rooms—except for Victoria, whom she asked to stay with Lucinda—until further notice. Victoria was more than happy to oblige. She was terribly concerned about Lucinda.

Lucinda's lucidity came and went. It wasn't certain whether her head had been injured in the attack, or if she was just distraught and weak. The school doctor and his nurse came to take care of Lucinda. Victoria sat in a chair in the corner of the room while Dr. Keating, the school doctor, and his nurse tended to Lucinda's needs.

Lucinda's injuries were more emotional than physical, even though she had lost consciousness from being strangled. Her appearance was deceiving; she looked worse than she actually was. Her neck was terribly bruised. The vessels in her eyes had burst. Her lip was swollen and split. There was blood on her face, neck, and bodice. Lucinda's hair was filthy and messy, and her clothes were soiled and torn.

Dr. Keating and his nurse cleaned Lucinda's wounds and checked her for broken bones. When Dr. Keating finally determined that Lucinda was physically all right, he sent for the headmistress.

Sylvia Dalton came to Lucinda's room. "Dr. Keating, how is she?"

"Let's step outside, shall we?" The doctor took Ms. Dalton by the elbow and led her into the hall. "Headmistress, Lucinda appears to be fine. Her physical injuries are minor, however, I'm sure she is very emotionally distraught. I would make sure she is not alone for the next few days; she's going to need support. I have taken care of her medical needs. You should have someone give her a bath. Have you sent for her family? I think it would be good for her to have family near."

"I understand. I will have the staff draw her a bath immediately. Victoria will probably want to stay with her; they are very close. As far as family, Aleister Wellington is her benefactor and fiancé. I have already sent for him. Thank you, doctor."

Ms. Dalton had two of the maids bring up a large metal tub and fill it with hot water. Victoria lay in the bed along with Lucinda while the bath was prepared. Lucinda lay with her head against Victoria's chest, while Victoria stroked Lucinda's hair. Neither girl said anything. They could tell the bath was ready when they smelled the sweet scent of peonies from the scented oil dropped into the hot water. The maids walked to the bed to help Lucinda. They helped her out of her undergarments and into the metal tub.

"What are you going to do with those?" Lucinda asked, as one of the maids gathered the dress and undergarments.

"We will clean and mend them," she said, wondering why Lucinda would ask a question with such an obvious answer.

"Please don't bother. Please just burn them. I don't want to see them again. You can understand why, I'm sure."

"Of course. As you wish." The maid left the room with the soiled garments.

Victoria dismissed the other maid and said she could help Lucinda. Victoria soaped a washcloth and washed Lucinda carefully.

Lucinda decided to ask how they came to find her and what had happened to the stable hand.

Victoria explained, "We realized you weren't in the building and began to look for you. We found you at the stables, unconscious. We all thought you were dead. We were so frightened."

"What of the stable hand, did you catch him?"

Victoria looked at Lucinda, puzzled. "Well, yes, of course. He was dead when we arrived —murdered, actually. Someone had beaten him to death. We were scarcely sure who he was at first."

"Someone murdered him? But why?"

"Apparently, to save your life."

"Maybe the murderer thought I was already dead."

"I suppose that could be the case."

"Well, I can't say that I am sorry. He got what he deserved." Lucinda was so upset that she blurted out something unintended. "I was terrified, once again being attacked. Only this time I thought for sure he would have is way with me, and leave me for dead." She realized too late what she had revealed. She only hoped she would not be pressed to explain.

"Again? You've been attacked before?"

"Yes—I'm sorry, I didn't mean to tell you. I never wanted it to be public. Please keep it to yourself. And please, don't ask me to explain."

Victoria looked into Lucinda's eyes and said, "I don't want you to tell me anything you do not want to. But you can tell me anything you need to. If you ever want or need to tell me more, you can. I will listen and be sympathetic, but I will not judge. You are my friend—my family."

Lucinda felt a great sense of relief. "Aleister knows everything. That's all I want to say about it."

Victoria kissed Lucinda on the forehead. "Very well."

Victoria coaxed Lucinda to lean back in the tub so she could wash Lucinda's hair. After Lucinda was clean, she relaxed in the warm water while Victoria sat on a stool beside the tub. They talked a bit. By the time the bathwater was cool, Lucinda felt much better, emotionally.

Chapter 10

When Aleister Wellington received the news about Lucinda, he was on his way to work. When he opened the door to leave, one of the servants from the school, Mary Roberts, was there, about to knock on the door. He immediately recognized her from the day before. "What is it? Lucinda? Is she all right?" He was panicked.

"I'm not sure. I know she has been hurt, and there was a murder. The headmistress sent for you and an inspector. Headmistress Dalton said to come right away. Shall I wait, or will you bring your own carriage?" Mary said as she handed him the note from Ms. Dalton that simply said there had been an incident, Lucinda needed him and to come quickly.

Dr. Wellington quickly glanced at the note and then replied, "I will ride with you. There is no time to wait."

Dr. Wellington called for Ms. Poe. He quickly explained what little he knew, and told her to prepare the carriage and some luggage. They would be staying at the Lady Kingston's for a while. Ms. Poe did as she was instructed.

Dr. Wellington went on ahead of Ms. Poe. However, Ms. Poe made haste and wasn't far behind the doctor.

Sylvia met Aleister at the door. She knew he would be

concerned and anxious to see Lucinda.

"Where is she, cousin?" he asked.

"Aleister, she is all right. I need to tell you what happened before you go to her. Do you trust me?"

"Of course I do, that's why I brought her to you."

"Then sit while I explain." They went into the parlor and sat across from one another. She relayed the events of Lucinda's encounter, in as much detail as she could, to the doctor.

"I have to see her." He didn't wait for a response. He immediately bounded up the stairs and to Lucinda's room. He burst through the door.

A wet and naked Lucinda, still in the tub, was terribly startled, as was Victoria. Victoria grabbed a large towel to cover Lucinda. Lucinda, with the help of Victoria, covered herself as Victoria helped her out of the tub.

"Aleister." Lucinda quietly said with a trembling voice and tear filled eyes.

Aleister rushed over to make sure Lucinda was indeed unharmed. Victoria took the cue and left.

"I would have never left you alone here, had I thought for one second you would not be safe. I shall never let you from my sight again."

"How could you have known? I place no blame on you."

"Lucinda Belle, I love you. I promised you I would never let anyone hurt you, and yet I was the one who lead you to the slaughter."

"I think that is a little dramatic. There was no slaughter. I am fine."

"You know what I mean. I left you here, and in less than a day, you were assaulted."

"This incident was unpredictable. And the offender is now dead." Lucinda stated plainly trying to command composure. She didn't want to upset Aleister any more than he already was by breaking down and crying.

"That is both disturbing and puzzling. Who murdered him, why, and why did they not harm you? And how did they know you were in harm's way in the first place?"

"That is curious."

"I'm taking you back with me after you have had a few

days to recover."

"I don't want to go back to the mansion. Is it possible for us to go back to the cottage, just for a while?"

"We can stay at the cottage. But I will try to find a more suitable home for us. I don't want to take you back to the mansion."

Lucinda smiled and felt comforted that Aleister was there, that he had rushed to be by her side. But she had grown tired again, and asked Aleister to let her rest. He stayed with her until she nodded off. When she was asleep, he went to find Ms. Dalton.

When Aleister found Sylvia, she was in one of the classrooms speaking to an instructor. She cut her conversation short and came out to speak with him.

"Aleister, how is she? I feel so badly about this situation. I did not give her permission to go to the stables, and even if I had, I definitely would not have allowed it before anyone else was awake to accompany her. I do feel responsible for Roy's actions, though. For that, I am truly sorry. I hope you can forgive me."

"Cousin, I do not hold you responsible for anyone else's actions—not Lucinda's, and definitely not the stable hand's. She seems fine, especially considering what she went through. Can I confide something to you?"

The sadness in his eyes concerned his cousin. "Of course. You can trust me. How many secrets have I kept for you from childhood—many are quite disturbing."

"Ah, yes. I know. Shall we not go into the past, though?"

"I didn't mean to offend. I just wanted you know I am loyal to you. What is troubling you?"

"This is not the first time Lucinda has been attacked by a man. The first time she was attacked no one came to her rescue and she had to fend for herself and was able to escape with her virtue. I made a vow to keep her safe, and I let her down. I brought her here to protect her from the evil at the mansion, and led her right into the lion's den."

"Aleister, to be fair, nothing of this nature has ever happened here before. You know the school has an impeccable reputation."

"I know. It's just that, she didn't want to come here. It's as if she knew something was amiss." He sighed, as if regretful.

"She has not been at the mansion for the past few weeks. Has the activity subsided since her absence?"

"I have been told yes. And everything was quiet last night. Let me ask you something, do you have any idea who might have murdered your stable hand?"

Sylvia shook her head. "I know of no one, nor any reason, other than to protect Lucinda."

Aleister sighed.

The headmistress continued, "The inspector is at the stables now, searching for evidence and taking statements. Speaking of which, have they any suspects in the murder of poor Emma Bronze?"

"No one in particular, and no real evidence."

The two cousins walked around the grounds, discussing plans for Lucinda. Finally, Aleister asked to see the stables. Sylvia escorted him. When he arrived, he found the inspector and his men still there, working. His eyes first caught sight of the rope Lucinda had been tied with.

He leaned over and touched it in regret. "Is this..."

Sylvia's voice was quiet. "Yes."

He then turned to look at the body of the murdered stable hand, which was covered by a linen sheet. He pulled the sheet back and gasped at the site. "This is repulsive."

"I know. He was beaten with that stick over there," she said. She pointed at a large piece of wood lying about five feet from the body.

Aleister's face grew red. "This bastard got what he deserved. I mean, after what he did—or tried to do—to Lucinda, to be honest, I think whoever did this to him should be honored. I hope the inspector fails in this investigation."

"Aleister! Don't speak that way—at least, not in front of the inspector and his men." Sylvia hushed him and ushered him away by the arm. "Come, cousin, you've seen quite enough." Once they were in a private place on the grounds, Sylvia let her cousin speak freely.

"May I speak my mind now?"

"Of course. I just don't want them to suspect you had anything to do with this. To be honest, your relationship is quite scandalous already, and it was even before your engagement. If I didn't know you so well, I might think you somehow stumbled upon the attack and lost your mind in a fit of rage. Does that sound conceivable to you?"

Aleister Wellington bowed his head in shame. "Yes. I am just outraged at the attack on Lucinda, and it appears all the inspector is concerned with is who killed the would-be rapist."

"I know. But with any luck, whoever did this aimed to protect Lucinda. If he merely left Lucinda for dead, you may want the person caught. He may come back to finish what he started."

"I had not considered that. I plan to stay here at least a week to be with Lucinda. I didn't want to just rush in and remove here hastily. I wanted to give her a few days to calm and recuperate. My plan was to take her back to the cottage. Has Ms. Poe arrived yet? I totally forgot about her."

Sylvia answered, "Yes. She is already settled into one of the rooms upstairs. We are treating her as a guest. Is that acceptable?"

"Actually, yes. She is more like family to me than help. She and Lucinda have become very close. I'm sure she will try to care for Lucinda. And I think I will watch Lucinda as close as possible. With your permission, I would like to stay in her room—as protection."

"I have already set up a room across the hall from

Lucinda for you. But I really didn't expect you to sleep there. However, you must keep up pretenses. I don't want to lose my position, and this is a respectable school."

Aleister nodded in agreement. "I understand. I will be discreet."

"Thank you."

A servant came to inform Sylvia Dalton that lunch was prepared, and all the girls were seated—with the exception of Victoria and Lucinda.

"Thank you," Sylvia told the servant. "Hold the meal, and I will be there shortly. Also, please set a place for Ms. Poe. She will be joining us for lunch."

"Yes, ma'am." The servant sped off to carry out Sylvia's orders.

Dr. Wellington returned to Lucinda's room to find her already up and getting dressed, with the help of Ms. Poe and Victoria. He was pleased to see her up. "Well, you recovered quickly enough." He smiled at Lucinda. Then he looked at Ms. Poe. "And it didn't take you long to find her, did it?"

"I feel like she is my own. I needed to care for her," Mrs. Poe replied.

"I cannot say this displeases me. Thank you, Ms. Poe. Ladies, lunch is being served. "Lucinda I will have someone bring our lunch up to us and we can eat here," Aleister suggested.

"Actually, I would rather go down and try to get my mind off of everything," Lucinda said.

"Well then ladies, shall I escort you to the dining hall?" The two girls started out of the room, and Ms. Poe stayed behind. Dr. Wellington paused and turned, "Ms. Poe are you not joining us?"

"Me, sir? In the dining hall?"

"Headmistress Dalton has asked to treat you as a guest. So, will you please join us?" Dr. Wellington didn't think he had ever seen Ms. Poe smile so brightly before. This warmed his heart. He escorted all three to lunch.

There was an uncomfortable silence in the dining hall that day. Every so often, Lucinda would notice one of the girls staring at her with sympathetic eyes. She knew that she was being pitied and she always hated that. Only at this moment she didn't care, though, because her lover was there to protect her. However, she wasn't looking forward to spending the night alone, unable to be with him. Dr.

Wellington had not yet informed her of the sleeping arrangements.

Her throat was sore from the strangulation. It hurt to swallow, and when she spoke it was raspy. She didn't eat very much; she wasn't very hungry. Even though she had wanted to eat in the dining hall, she was relieved when the meal concluded. She wanted to be alone with Aleister. As he pulled her chair out for her, she asked if they could take a private walk.

"I will do anything you ask of me. If you wish to walk about the grounds privately, then that is what we shall do." He laced her arm through his and led her outside into the cool, brisk afternoon.

Once they were alone, Lucinda spoke. "It's a strange thing. This morning, I couldn't sleep, so I came out to be with Lady Jane. The morning was beautiful, and my life finally had purpose and meaning. The day had many prospects. Then I found myself in the stables with my life flashing before my eyes. Everything turned black. I feared I would never see your face again. Then I woke up in the arms of Headmistress Dalton. At first, I thought I had died. But as I regained my senses, I knew God had found it in his heart to give me another chance. Then you arrived to be with me. We are walking together about these beautiful grounds, and my life once again is charmed. Once again, this is a beautiful day with many prospects."

Dr. Wellington cried openly. He held Lucinda and wept on her shoulder. She stroked his hair and comforted him. She couldn't believe such a strong man could be made so weak by her love.

"Aleister, I am fine. I am here. We are together. Please, don't cry."

He stood up and tried his best to compose himself. After a few minutes, he was able to bring his weeping to a halt. He felt embarrassed for breaking down in front of Lucinda, but he couldn't help it. His emotions took hold of him. "I know. I just feel so guilty. I vowed to keep you safe, and you had to endure such a horrible thing. I should have kept you with me. I am sorry. Can you ever forgive me?"

"There is nothing to forgive. You did not put me in harm's way. I should not have come out so early by myself. I was instructed not to leave the house without permission. I was defiant, and that put me in peril—not your actions. I love you. I am happy to see you. I am thrilled you are here."

They went about their day, enjoying one another's

company. The inspector and his men finally finished their investigation and left, taking the corpse with them. The headmistress announced that classes would not resume until Monday, which would give the girls several days of free time. When the day finally came to an end, everyone retired to their rooms for the night. Aleister Wellington escorted Lucinda to her room. He kissed her at the door.

"I will dream of you tonight, Aleister. Please dream of me." She turned to go into her room and was surprised when he followed her in. "What are you doing? You're not supposed to be in here."

"You should realize by now that I have special privileges here." He pushed the door closed behind him and smiled.

Lucinda was happy to see him smile. He seemed to be more like himself.

Aleister helped her change into her nightgown.

Lucinda wearily climbed into bed exhausted from the day's events. Aleister walked over to the settee next to the window he pulled his boots off and lay back to settle in for the night.

"What are you doing over there?" Lucinda asked.

"I'm sleeping over here tonight. I wanted to give you some space. I didn't want you to be alone tonight but I didn't want to make you uncomfortable either."

"Oh Aleister, I need you to be by my side. I need you to hold me and make me feel safe tonight. Please sleep over here with me," Lucinda pleaded.

"Only if you're certain."

"I am," Lucinda said with a tired smile.

Aleister was relieved that she wanted and needed him so close. He slid under the covers beside her. Lucinda snuggled in a closely as possible. She needed to feel his strong loving embrace. She needed to feel safe. And in Aleister's arms was where she felt the safest.

They fell asleep in one another's arms. Lucinda dreamt of the strangest things that night.

Chapter 11

Lucinda wandered through the back alleys of Whitechapel in the pitch-black night. She could hear a couple of prostitutes conducting business. She remembered that one lonely and fearful night she had spent in the alley. Lucinda thought about how lucky she was— how easily it could have been her conducting "business." She then heard a horrific scream. Lucinda ran toward the terrifying sound.

By the time Lucinda reached the woman, it was too late. There was no hope for the poor whore. Lucinda stopped short, to avoid being seen by the one who had stifled the life from the hapless victim. The worst was still to come. He cut her throat; even in the night, Lucinda could see the woman being mutilated. Lucinda was horrified, but could not avert her eyes. She found herself with a morbid fascination with what was being done to the corpse. The woman was already dead. There was nothing Lucinda could do to help, anyway. So, she looked on as the murderer cut and sliced, until most of her internal organs had been ripped out, including reproductive organs. The murderer sliced through her flesh, exposing yellow fat and bones.

When the mutilator turned, Lucinda could not distinguish much—only that the figure somehow resembled the shadow she had seen her first night at Dr. Wellington's mansion. The only thing distinguishable was a pair of piercing eyes. Suddenly, the murderer darted toward Lucinda. She felt like her feet were planted to the ground. She could not move. She screamed out.

"Lucinda. Lucinda, wake up. It is only a dream. You're safe. I am here. No one can harm you."

Lucinda opened her eyes to find herself still in the arms of her wonderful Dr. Wellington at Lady Kingston's. It was the middle of the night. She sobbed uncontrollably. He held her tightly and stroked her hair. He kept whispering to her over and over that she was safe.

"It was terrible. I was in the back alleys of Whitechapel and witnessed a prostitute being murdered. She was cut up like Emma. I couldn't see, but the murderer looked like the shadow I saw the first night at the mansion. When it finished with her, it came at me. Oh, Aleister, why should I have such a troubling dream?" Lucinda's weeping subsided.

"It's okay. It was probably because of everything that happened yesterday. It was just a dream. Don't worry. Try to get some sleep. Come closer and let me hold you. You know you are safe with me, don't you?" Aleister pulled Lucinda as close as he could and held her tightly.

"I know. But the dream was so real. That spirit at the mansion is so evil. Could it possibly find away out of the mansion? I am sure it had something to do with Emma's death."

"Lucinda, there is an evil presence at the mansion, and maybe it did have a hand in poor Mrs. Bronze's murder, but I highly doubt it could leave. There is no reason to be concerned. Please, just try to sleep. Everything will be fine in the light of day. You'll see."

Lucinda lay close to Aleister, but did not sleep very well. She couldn't shake the uneasy feeling about her nightmare.

That morning when the she heard the cock's crow, she did not want to get out of bed. Her only desire at that moment was to be right where she was, in her fiancé's arms, safe and happy. She lay there for several hours before he awoke. Aleister could see she had been awake for a while.

"How do you feel this morning?"

"I have been laying here for hours, and all I can think about is that nightmare. I am still very shaken, and I still think there was more to the dream."

"Let's not worry about that right now. Let's discuss our

future. I obviously cannot stay here at the school with you, and you cannot go back to the mansion—especially now. I suppose we can go back to the cottage until I can find an interested party in the mansion. But soon, I will find you a new home—one you fall in love with, one you cannot live without. We will marry soon and you will come to live in that home—our home."

Lucinda didn't know what to say. This was what she wanted. But it wasn't what Aleister wanted for her. Since he had come into her life, he had protected her and cared for her—she knew he would be always be there. As badly as she wanted to stay with him and never leave his side, she knew her education was so important to him. She could not answer right away. This was something she would have to ponder extensively.

"What? No answer?"

"No. I just want to settle my mind, ponder over some issues and possible solutions. Can you give me a few days to think about our future?"

"Of course. I think it's time we got dressed and went down for breakfast. Come." He got out of bed and gently tugged at her until she got up as well. Aleister went to his room to change clothes and left Lucinda to change into hers.

When he had changed, he went back to Lucinda's room and knocked on the door lightly. Lucinda answered already completely dressed. They went downstairs and dined privately with Ms. Dalton in the gardens.

"Well, cousin, have you heard from the inspector yet? Do they have any suspects?" Dr. Wellington asked.

"I have not heard a word from the inspector. However, I did get a letter from Melinda Whitman this morning. She was concerned about Victoria. She thinks the murder of Emma Bronze and the murder that happened here may be connected."

"Why would she consider that?" Lucinda asked.

"I'm not sure. It was a suspicious letter, though. Would you like to read it? You two may find something I missed."

"Yes, please." Dr. Wellington reached out his hand as she pulled the letter from her pocket.

Dr. Wellington opened the letter, and he and Lucinda read it together.

Dear Headmistress Dalton,

I hope my letter finds you well in light of recent circumstances. I am writing to make sure my daughter's safety is being secured. She has been present at both murders, as has Lucinda Belle. I fear these two tragedies may be related in some manner—the way the bodies were mangled. Please keep a watchful eye on my daughter. I suppose my concern for her is so strong due to my husband's constant absence. He spends much of his time away from home. It is natural for me to feel insecure. Please watch over my daughter and give her my love.

Yours Truly,

Melinda Whitman

After he finished reading, Aleister said, "I think there is a hidden message in Mrs. Whitman's letter."

"Well, you cannot just tell me you have found a hidden message and leave it at that. I am much too curious. Tell me, Aleister."

"I must have your word that what we share you will keep in strict confidence. I know that if you give me your word, I can trust you to honor it."

"Of course, Aleister. And if one of my girls is in

possible danger, I need to know."

He nodded and said, "Melinda Whitman thinks the judge is capable of unspeakable acts. She knows for certain of at least one attack. He also had an intimate relationship with Emma Bronze at one point. He was unaccounted for at the time of the murder."

"I wouldn't put anything past that brute," Sylvia declared. "Was there anyone else unaccounted for that night?"

"Well, Lucinda and I were each alone for a short time. But we were together when we heard Ms. Poe scream the first time. Actually, we bumped into the judge just before the second scream, and then we three found Melinda wandering around. I don't know about any of the other guests. Why do you ask?"

Sylvia shrugged. "Just wondering—you know how a woman scorned can be."

"You don't think Melinda is capable of such an atrocity, do you?" Aleister asked.

"Women are capable of many things, cousin. So, can you tell me who the judge was accused of attacking? Has this woman come to a terrible end yet, or do we know?" Sylvia asked.

Lucinda's eyes instantly began to water. It was very hard to hold the tears back. In an instant, Sylvia knew Lucinda had been the victim. She remembered her conversation with her cousin the day before, when he had confided in her about Lucinda's first assault.

She said, "I'm so sorry. I had no idea."

"That's alright," Lucinda said, sniffling.

Lucinda let Aleister explain everything about the attack—starting from her attack, and ending with Melinda's discovery of it. Aleister left no detail out.

When he was finished, Sylvia spoke. "I don't want to alarm you, but did you think that there may be more in common with the two murders? Emma and Lucinda both had a past with the judge. It is possible that Roy was not the intended victim. Maybe the murderer was interrupted before the intended task—killing Lucinda—was completed. Is it possible that Melinda could be the murderer, and she wanted to frame her husband?"

"Or maybe the letter is of genuine concern, and the judge is to blame." Aleister put his arm around Lucinda to comfort her.

"In either case, we must be watchful over Lucinda. I think we should also contact Inspector Anderson and let him in on when we have surmised."

"James Lawrence is already working with the inspector regarding the suspicions about Judge Whitman. Melinda went to him before she came to us." Aleister explained.

"I still believe it is possible that Melinda could be the murderer, because her husband enjoyed the taste of forbidden fruit."

"I will send word to Inspector Anderson to come here. We will discuss our suspicions with him then. Can one of your staff accompany Ms. Poe into town to deliver the note?"

"Of course, I will arrange it right away. Compose your letter, and have Ms. Poe prepare to depart." Sylvia briskly walked back to the house.

"Aleister, I cannot believe it was Mrs. Whitman. She always treated me well. I feel she genuinely cared for me." Lucinda said.

"That may be true. But it may be that she is the murderer, and her intent was not to harm you, but to incriminate her husband by killing Emma and the stable hand in the same manner. Or, she is being honest with us, and she does suspect her husband is the murderer. Either way, I feel you are in possible danger."

"This I have not disputed."

They spent the afternoon sitting in the parlor, relaxing and talking. Ms. Poe had not been gone long before she returned. And she returned with Inspector Anderson.

Dr. Wellington, Lucinda, and Ms. Dalton greeted the inspector. Aleister shook his hand and said, "Inspector Anderson, thank you for coming. I did not expect you to come so quickly, though."

They all went into the parlor. The headmistress told the staff they were not to be disturbed under any circumstances. She closed the door and locked it, putting the key in her pocket. They all sat. Ms. Dalton and Dr. Wellington wasted no time explaining their suspicions and theories. They showed him the letter from Ms. Whitman.

The inspector explained that he had already considered Melinda Whitman a suspect. Due to the judge's indiscretions, she could have been motivated by jealousy. He also told them that, when he heard about the murder at Lady Kingston's, he was immediately suspicious that the two incidents were related due to the nature of the crimes. But he had no news to report pertaining to Emma's murder.

The inspector left, and the next few days were uneventful. The nights, however, were quite the opposite. Dr. Wellington discreetly spent the nights with Lucida. Soon, it was Monday, and classes resumed as Headmistress Dalton had instructed. Lucinda decided to attend classes. She was there, anyway, and it would be a couple of days before Aleister was to leave and she too, if that were her decision.

To her surprise, Lucinda enjoyed the classes. She was allowed to speak her mind and debate with like-minded women. This was a wonderful feeling. She had never felt so intellectually liberated. By the end of the day, she had reconsidered staying on at Lady Kingston's.

After her last class, she found Aleister waiting in her room. "Did you enjoy yourself today?" he asked. "Actually, I did, but you know that already. You weren't at all discreet today, following me and observing. I did enjoy the discussions and debates. I have never been encouraged to be self-expressive—except with you. But that does not count, because you are my lover, and you are nothing if not encouraging."

"I am happy you enjoyed yourself. I thought you would enjoy it here. I am just sorry things did not work out as I had hoped."

Lucinda walked over to Aleister, who was sitting on her bed. She stood between his legs and wrapped her arms around his neck. She leaned in and kissed him deeply. "I do so love you."

"I have no doubt. I love you as much."

"And that I have never doubted. I hope you won't think badly of me if I have a request."

"I would never think badly of you. I would grant you any request in my power; you know that. What is it that you wish, Lucinda Belle?"

"I think I would like to stay here and continue my education, as you originally desired. I would much rather be with you and be your wife. But I have never had this type of freedom to learn. I thought the education here would be just in etiquette, I did not realize that there would be so much more involved. It is rather exhilarating. Would you be opposed to it?"

"I am the one who wanted you to be educated here in the first place. However, there is the concern of your safety, and I have become accustomed to spending the nights with you. If I agree to this, you have to agree to stipulations."

"What are your terms?" Lucinda asked.

"First of all, you will never leave this house without at least one other person to accompany you. Secondly, you must come with me each weekend to the cottage. I know I cannot be without you longer than five days. Agreed?"

"Are you certain?"

"I am. You will be happy here. I believe these arrangements will be more agreeable to us than the original arrangement. You still get your education here at Lady Kingston's, and yet we have each and every weekend together." Aleister pulled her closer and kissed her. She could feel his smile through his kiss. She loved when he did that. "Very well, then. We should see Sylvia and let her know of our plans. Shall we go now?"

"Please. That would be wonderful."

They informed Sylvia Dalton of their intentions. She was happy to know Lucinda would be staying. Aleister stayed until the end of the week with Lucinda. He took her back to the cottage for the weekend, and on Sunday evening she returned to Lady Kingston's.

Lucinda and Victoria were becoming ever closer. Lucinda enjoyed this arrangement so much, she almost forgot about the murders, the mansion, the nightmares, and everything that had once weighed so heavy upon her heart—until she was called from class by the headmistress one afternoon.

Chapter 12

"Lucinda, I need to speak with you please. It is urgent." Sylvia Dalton looked very upset. Lucinda could not imagine what was wrong.

"Headmistress, what is it?" Lucinda left her chair to walk with Ms. Dalton to her office.

As they walked, Ms. Dalton said, "What I need to tell you is very private." When they reached Ms. Dalton's office, she closed the door and gestured for Lucinda to take a seat. "There has been another murder. Very similar to that of Emma Bronze and Roy's."

"Where? When? Who?" That was all that Lucinda could manage.

"The murder victim was a prostitute in Whitechapel. She was found in the back alleys of Whitechapel this morning. She was mutilated in the same manner as the others. Her name is Mary Nichols."

Lucinda immediately remembered her nightmare about the murder and mutilation of a prostitute.

The horrified look on Lucinda's face let Ms. Dalton know there was something more bothering Lucinda. "What is it, Lucinda?"

"Well, I had a dream right after my attack about the murder of a prostitute in a back alley of Whitechapel. Did Aleister mention that to you?"

"No, he didn't. That is bizarre." She looked at Lucinda, puzzled, not knowing what to say. After a long, uncomfortable pause, she continued to explain more about the murder. "This murder was slightly different, in that Mary Nichols had grapes in her hand and wine on her breath."

In an instant Lucinda remembered how Aleister had given her grapes and wine in the carriage the day he found her. That was very coincidental. A terrible thought came to her; what if someone suspected Aleister? She knew he was innocent, but would others? She tried to keep her composure as thoughts flooded her mind. "That is strange. Why would a prostitute have grapes and wine?"

"The inspectors speculate she was lured away by the murderer, enticing her with grapes and wine. That is not important. The important thing is you must be cautious and stay with someone at all times. I am going to ask that Victoria stay with you at night. Do you object?"

"No, not at all. I would actually rest better with

company, knowing there has been another murder. Thank you, Headmistress."

"Off you go, then. Return to class. I will see you at dinner. And Lucinda, be safe."

"I will. Thank you."

Chapter 13

The inspector alerted Dr. Wellington of the most recent murder by way of messenger. Aleister wasted no time informing Ms. Poe of an immediate trip to Lady Kingston's. "Ms. Poe, please prepare clothing enough for us both for at least three days. We will be leaving right away."

"Yes, sir. Has something else happened? Is Lucinda alright?" Ms. Poe asked, while wringing her hands in worry.

"Oh, Ms. Poe. I'm so sorry. I didn't mean to alarm you." He reached over and took her wrinkled hands in his young, strong hands.

"Lucinda is just fine. However, there has been another murder, very similar to the other two. This time, the victim was a prostitute. I just want to be certain Lucinda is safe. I'm certain she will be upset by the news."

Ms. Poe was relieved to know Lucinda was all right, but alarmed at the news of another murder. She prepared their things, and they made haste to Lady Kingston's.

Inspector Anderson made a surprise visit to Judge Whitman's home. He wanted to inform the Whitmans personally of the most recent murder. He was anxious to witness their reaction firsthand.

The inspector knocked on the door of the Whitman home. One of the servants answered the door. It was Loraine, Mrs. Whitman's most trustworthy and faithful servant. She was both shocked and concerned to see the inspector at their door unexpectedly. "Good morning, sir. On whom are you calling today, sir?"

"Both Judge and Mrs. Whitman, please. Are they available?"

Before Loraine could answer, Melinda Whitman came to the door. "Who is it, Loraine?" She saw the inspector. "Oh, hello, inspector. What can I do for you this morning? Do have any word on Emma Bronze or the stable hand's murder yet?"

"Not exactly. Is your husband home?"

"Inspector you are beginning to cause me great concern. Has something happened to my daughter?" Melinda looked as though she may faint at any minute.

"No, Mrs. Whitman. It's nothing like that. I have heard nothing about your daughter. However, there has been another murder. It was in town and the victim was a prostitute. I would just like to ask you and your husband a few questions, if I may. Is he home?"

"Yes. Please come inside and have a seat." Melinda led him into the parlor and gestured to a lovely chair across from where she sat.

Melinda then instructed Loraine to retrieve her husband from his study. "Would you like to speak with me while we are waiting, or do you want to speak to us together?"

"I would prefer together, so I only explain things once."

"Very well. I don't think Isaiah is busy, so he shouldn't be long. Would you like some tea while you're waiting?"

"No, thank you. "

Judge Whitman stormed into the room. It was obvious he was not happy to see the inspector. "Inspector."

"I regret intruding upon you today, but there has been yet another murder. It is very similar to the others. It occurred last night. I am speaking with several people who were at the doctor's ball. I just need to ask you and your wife a few questions."

"Questions? About what?"

"Well, is there anything you might be able to tell me

about where you were last night? Did you see or hear anything, if you were out late?"

"This line of questioning is suspicious. You don't think either of us had anything to do with the murder, do you?" Judge Whitman demanded.

"Judge, I am not accusing anyone of anything. I am only trying to see if we can make connections between the murders. I need to know if you were alone or not. I'm certain your wife was with you, am I correct?"

"Yes," the judge snapped.

Melinda interrupted. "Actually, I went to bed early. Isaiah didn't come to bed until much later. I am sure he was here in the house. He just wasn't with me."

Judge Whitman grew angrier by the second. His face turned red, his eyes bulged, and the veins in his face and neck began to swell. He wrung his hands. "I was here the entire night." He growled the words through his teeth.

"Judge, can anyone substantiate your whereabouts?"

"I'm sure one of my servants can vouch for me."

"Your staff may vouch for you, but can anyone else give you an alibi?"

"No." It was all the judge could do to control his temper.

"Mrs. Whitman, can you account for your whereabouts last night?" the inspector continued. "As I said, I went to bed before my husband. I did, however, receive a late visit from a good friend, Lady Fleming. She came by at about ten o'clock to gossip."

"What was so important that she felt the need to gossip so late in the evening?" asked the inspector. "Dr. Wellington's engagement to Lucinda Belle." Mrs. Whitman answered with a smirk. Judge Whitman stormed from the room. The mere mention of Lucinda's name sent him into a rage.

"Is your husband alright?" Inspector Anderson asked.

"Yes. He's just a bit touchy."

"Why did Lady Fleming need to gossip about Dr. Wellington at that hour?"

"She is very upset. Lord Fleming and Dr. Wellington are very close friends, and Lady Fleming was certain Dr. Wellington would ask for the hand of her daughter, Miranda. Lady Fleming was also upset that he had become engaged to a servant girl he barely knew, and that Lucinda was now attending the same school as Miranda."

"What was your response to that?"

"Lady Fleming is a dear, old friend. However, I love Lucinda like a daughter, and I am very happy for her. I tried to convince Lady Fleming to reconsider her opinion. I defended the doctor and Lucinda. She was upset, but we still parted as friends."

"Thank you, I will speak to Lady Fleming later today."

"She can corroborate my story. Just out of curiosity, what time was the prostitute murdered?"

"We believe she expired around 9:30 or 10:00. So, obviously, if Lady Fleming's accounts of last evening agrees with yours, you will no longer be a suspect."

"I understand completely."

"Thank you, Mrs. Whitman. I can see myself out. If you can think of anything that might assist in the investigation, please let me know."

"I will. Thank you, inspector."

Inspector Anderson left. As soon as the door had closed, the judge let his rage free. He took his anger out on his wife. He grabbed Melinda by both arms and squeezed. She cried out in pain. Through clinched teeth, he threatened Melinda, "I should kill you where you stand. I am your husband, and you are bound to me—to stand by me, no matter what. You can't even give me an alibi. Why? Would you have me convicted of these murders so that I should hang? You could then have my fortune to yourself."

Melinda winced in pain. "I couldn't cover for you. Apparently, you weren't eavesdropping closely enough. Lady Fleming was here. She knew you weren't with me. So, what good would it have done for me to lie to the inspector?"

The enraged judge drew one hand back to strike her. He propelled his fist at her face with all the force he had. He hit her in the mouth so hard that one of her teeth pierced her lip, while another tooth was completely knocked out. She fell to the ground and did not stir.

Luckily, Melinda's faithful servant, Loraine, heard what was happening and ran out to retrieve the inspector before he could leave.

Judge Whitman picked up a heavy, silver candlestick and drew it back. He was so furious; he wanted Melinda dead and out of his life forever. Just before he struck the final blow, the inspector grabbed his hand. The judged could not contain his rage. He turned to attack the inspector. Inspector Anderson pulled his revolver on Judge Whitman. The temperament of the judge immediately became solemn. He dropped the candlestick and sat down on a nearby chair.

"Judge Whitman, I am placing you under arrest for the assault and attempted murder of your wife." Inspector Anderson then turned to Loraine and told her to fetch a doctor for Mrs. Whitman.

The doctor who lived next door to the Whitmans arrived within minutes. He greeted the inspector and promptly attended to Melinda Whitman.

"Doctor, I am going to take Judge Whitman to the station. I will be back soon to check on Mrs. Whitman."

"Yes, sir." The doctor spoke over his shoulder, as he continued to care for Mrs. Whitman.

After the inspector had escorted Judge Whitman to a jail cell, he came back to the Whitman home to check on Melinda and to speak to the servants. They told Inspector Anderson what they had heard, and Loraine explained what she had seen.

After the doctor had tended to Melinda's wounds, Inspector Anderson questioned her about the argument that resulted in the assault. He then wished her well and bid her farewell. Loraine stayed with Melinda that night.

When Inspector Anderson arrived at work the next morning, he was surprised to find Judge Whitman was no longer in his cell. "Where is the judge?"

A fellow policeman answered the inspector's question, "He was released this morning."

"On whose orders? I, myself, witnessed him attack his wife."

"The orders came from Sir Charles Warren."

"The commissioner? Why?"

"The Judge has close ties with the royal family. Did you honestly think he would be held accountable?" The officer shrugged.

"I had hoped justice would be served. I must go to the Whitman's home to ensure Melinda is safe," Inspector Anderson called over his shoulder, as he darted out the door of the police station.

Melinda Whitman arose early to the sound of her husband knocking at her bedroom door. "Melinda. May I enter?"

Loraine was still with Melinda. Loraine looked at Melinda, questioning with her eyes. Melinda nodded her head yes. "I will let him in, but I will not leave this room, Mrs. Whitman."

"Thank you."

Loraine opened the door cautiously. "She is still resting, sir. She did not sleep well last night."

"Of course. I won't keep her long." He made his way past Loraine. "Melinda, I regret losing my temper last night. I regret that I mistreated you. Most of all, I regret being hauled away to jail. To ensure something like this does not occur in the future, I propose we keep our distance from one another. We still live in the same house, and share a daughter, so we must keep up appearances. Is this an agreeable arrangement?"

"Yes, Isaiah. This arrangement is for the best."

"Very well." The judge turned to walk away, but then stopped and turned back. "Oh, and Melinda, I have many friends in high places, and the events of last night will soon be forgotten."

Judge Whitman turned and left his wife's room. As he was walking back to his study, he heard one of the servants speaking to someone at the door. It was the unmistakable voice of Inspector Anderson. The judge changed his direction and went to greet the inspector. "Inspector, may I help you?"

"I just wanted to check in on your wife to see how she is feeling."

"Oh, come now, inspector. I think we both know why you are really here. You wanted to make sure I didn't finish what I started last night." The judge smiled coldly and gestured for the inspector to enter. "Well, don't just stand there. Come in. She is upstairs, second door on the left."

"Thank you." The inspector proceeded to Melinda's room. After seeing no further injuries and speaking with her for a few moments, he told her to let him know if she needed anything and left.

Chapter 14

Lucinda loved waking up next to Aleister. But she hated the reason he was there with her once again. She felt badly for Mary Nichols, and was fearful for herself and others. When would they catch this murderer? Why was this monster committing these horrible acts?

Aleister had been watching her sleep for a long while before she stirred. "How did you sleep?"

"Very well in your arms. However, I am still frightened from all these murders. When will the inspector let us know something?"

"When he has any news, he said we would be informed immediately. Don't worry. I will make certain you are kept safe."

Lucinda laid her head back against his chest and breathed deeply, inhaling his wonderful scent. It made her calm and comfortable. They eventually decided they must begin their day. Dr. Wellington headed into town to see a few patients, and Lucinda went to classes as usual.

The days passed uneventfully, and Dr. Wellington returned to his home while Lucinda continued classes at Lady Kingston's. After about a week, another prostitute, Annie

Chapman, was found murdered and mutilated.

Inspector Anderson went to Dr. Wellington's office to inform him of the latest murder. "Dr. Wellington, I hate to interrupt your busy schedule, but there has been another murder just last night. The victim was another prostitute. Commissioner Warren has requested Chief Inspector Donald Swanson to head the case."

"What does he think is the common factor in all the murders?" Dr. Wellington asked.

"Actually, he doesn't think there is a connection. His speculation is that Emma was murdered by a jealous lover, the stable hand got what he deserved, and someone else just wants to rid the streets of London of prostitutes. We received a letter today from someone claiming to be the murderer of the prostitutes. The letter was signed 'Jack the Ripper.' The stable hand's case has gone cold; the evidence has come to a standstill. I am being kept on Emma's case. And, as I said before, Chief Inspector Swanson has been assigned to the case of the prostitutes."

"But you still think the murders are related?"

"Yes. But my hands are tied. I am not to cross-investigate. I have been strictly instructed to work on my case, and only my case. I will keep you informed."

"What of Lucinda? Do you think she is safe at Lady Kingston's?"

"It appears the murderer has decided on a preference for a specific type of victim. Since Lucinda is not working the streets of London, I'm certain she is safe, far from the Ripper."

"Thank you, inspector. Please let me know if there is anything that I can do to help."

"I will. Good day, Dr. Wellington."

Dr. Wellington felt a bit more at ease, but the murders were still disconcerting. He stayed late in his office that night to work on a special project. It had been a while since he had a fresh cadaver to experiment on; he had spent a lot of time recently with Lucinda, and after the first Whitechapel murder, the police patrolled more at night, making it difficult for grave robbers.

He had forgotten how much he enjoyed his work. He became so engrossed in it that he totally lost track of time and worked all through the night. As the next few weeks passed, Dr. Wellington kept himself busy at nights in his secret laboratory, avoiding the mansion. Even though the activity in the mansion had lessened since Lucinda had left, in recent weeks the presence in the mansion had become more active, allowing no one in the house to sleep. It paced the house at night, casting shadows under doors and into rooms. The scratching grew more intense, and Dr. Wellington and his staff were being affected. Something whispered in their ears frequently.

About two weeks after the murder of Annie Chapman, two more women were found: Elizabeth Stride and Catherine Eddowes. They were murdered within an hour of one another. Once again, the women were found with their throats cut and their bodies badly mutilated.

Chapter 15

Lucinda was faring a bit better than Aleister. She was far from the mansion, and in fact had almost forgotten about it—until one night, when she had a nightmare. She dreamed she was in the mansion, in her room, and the spirit entered the room in the form of Aleister. It kissed her and turned into one of the cadavers from Aleister's lab. She awoke up in a cold sweat, screaming. No one in the house heard her but Victoria, since their rooms were so close.

Victoria rushed into the room to see what was the matter. "Lucinda, it's all right. It was only a dream. Would you like me to stay?"

"Yes, please." Lucinda finally calmed down. She was reassured having Victoria with her.

The two girls talked for quite a while. Victoria was such a comfort to Lucinda; they had become even closer than before in recent months. Victoria reassuringly tried to get Lucinda to rest.

Lucinda finally became so tired that she had no other choice but to sleep. "Victoria, will you promise not leave until I wake?"

"I promise. I am your friend and will always be your

friend. Friends watch over one another. I think you know I love you like a sister. I will stay while you sleep."

"And I love you. Thank you for being such a wonderful friend."

"Let's sleep now." Victoria said with a yawn.

Lucinda rolled over, and the two girls went to sleep. They awoke the next morning, got dressed and headed down to breakfast. Lucinda was still shaken by the nightmare but felt like she could face the day.

It had been a of couple weeks since the last murder in Whitechapel, and the girls had almost forgotten about the recent tragedies. However, at breakfast that morning, Headmistress Dalton received a letter from Inspector Anderson that read:

Headmistress Dalton,

I hope my letter finds you well. I don't mean to alarm you but, since I am still convinced Jack the Ripper's victims are related to the murders of Emma Bronze and the stable hand, I felt the need to inform you that there has been another murder. It occurred two nights ago. There were actually two murders in less than one hour— two more prostitutes, Elizabeth Stride and Catherine Eddowes. I just wanted to alert you to keep a close watch on your girls. Please feel free to contact me if you should need anything.

Thank you,

Inspector Anderson

Ms. Dalton shared the disturbing news with the students. She asked that no one leave the house alone, and that everyone sleep in pairs.

With the mention of this terrible news, Lucinda once again wondered if these murders had anything to do with the specter in the mansion. After all, that was where the first murder took place. Lucinda wondered if Aleister would come to check on her to ensure her safety. She waited all day, but Aleister never came. She wondered if he had heard the news, and if so, why he had not come to her.

At the end of the day, when Headmistress Dalton instructed the students to retire, Victoria asked Lucinda if she wanted her to stay with her.

"I really don't want to be alone with a murderer on the loose, even if he seems to be concentrating his activities in London. I would feel much safer if you stayed with me tonight."

They prepared for bed and retired almost immediately. The night was long for Lucinda. She tossed and turned and, once again, had nightmares about the mansion. Morning came not a minute to soon, even though she was so tired. Lucinda was concerned about Aleister. She couldn't wait to spend the weekend with him.

Lucinda carried on with classes and the days passed, and the weekend finally arrived.

Aleister arrived early, but he did not pull Lucinda from her classes. He spent the afternoon with Sylvia Dalton in the gardens.

"My dear cousin, Sylvia. I trust you heard the news of the latest murders in London?"

"Yes. Inspector Anderson sent a letter. I was disappointed to learn that he is not investigating those murders, as well. I do believe all the murders are related. Do you have any idea why the decision was made?"

Aleister answered, "There is gossip floating around that Judge Whitman attacked his wife and was arrested. However, he was released and everything was swept under the rug. I think he is suspect in all the murders, but someone high up is protecting him. If this is the case, and if Judge Whitman is guilty, then the murderer will never be brought to justice and the murders will never cease. I may have to take Lucinda and flee London in order to keep her safe."

"I understand. I can understand why the judge would be a suspect. He is such a brute."

"How has Lucinda been?"

"She and Victoria are inseparable, so you have no need to fear her being lonely. She has adjusted very well to life here at Lady Kingston's. She has become quite popular. There is something, though. It has nothing to do with Lucinda, but--"

"But what? Has something happened?" Aleister's voice rose in worry.

"It's just that, we think someone is either secretly entering or leaving the house at times. I'm certain it's not Lucinda. I think its probably one of the other girls, meeting a boy in some secret rendezvous. It's just, with the Whitechapel murders, I worry."

"I'm sure you're right. However, this does call for concern."

"I am going to hire someone to come and make certain the house is secure through the night," Sylvia assured him.

"Wonderful. That eases my mind greatly. I still intend to take her home with me this weekend, though," Aleister said.

"Well, cousin, I didn't think you came here today to leave empty-handed." Sylvia smiled.

The two cousins continued to talk until classes concluded for the day. Aleister met Lucinda in her room, where she was packing her things in anticipation of his arrival.

When Lucinda saw him, her heart leapt. She jumped into his arms and hugged him tightly around the neck. He held her close, and they kissed as if it were the last kiss they would ever have. After their passionate greeting, Lucinda asked, "Have you not heard of the latest murders in Whitechapel?"

Aleister admitted, "Yes. I have heard. The inspector came to inform me the morning after the bodies were found."

"I thought you would come." Lucinda looked very disappointed, and tears began to form in her eyes.

Aleister cupped her face with his hands. "I asked Inspector Anderson if he thought I should be concerned with your well-being here. He led me to believe you would be very safe here."

"Safe? There was a murder that occurred here, remember?"

Aleister explained, "The police commissioner has deemed that murder a terrible incident, but the evidence has led them nowhere, so it is not a priority at this point. Inspector Anderson is only investigating the murder of Emma Bronze. The commissioner is treating the murders in Whitechapel as a separate case. He has entrusted Chief Inspector Swanson with the lead in the Whitechapel murder investigation."

"So, are there suspects in Emma's murder?"

"No one has said it, but I believe Judge Whitman is the prime suspect, especially after he attacked his wife."

"He did what? Does Victoria know?"

"I don't know all the details, but I do know that the inspector arrested him, and that the commissioner released him. The charges will most likely be dropped, and the judge will probably be removed from the suspect list for Emma's murder. I don't know if Victoria is aware of anything."

"I'm certain she is not. She would have mentioned it to me." Lucinda declared.

"Yes, Sylvia said you two have become very close."

"We have always been close—we just feared the judge would discover our friendship and cast me out. Mrs. Whitman tried her best to protect me."

Aleister's eyes began to form tears, and he held Lucinda tightly. He kissed the top of her head and whispered, "You will never have to fear the judge, nor any man like him, again. I love you, Lucinda Belle."

"I love you, Aleister." Lucinda squeezed around his waist, as if he might disappear if she did not hold tight enough.

"Shall we finish packing your things? I have a small surprise for you." He smiled brightly, lightening the mood.

"What is it, Aleister?"

"If I told you, it would not be a surprise. Get your things packed, and you will see for yourself."

Lucinda made haste with her packing. He took her downstairs and out to his awaiting carriage. Lucinda's eyes widened, and she rushed to the carriage.

"Oh, Aleister, is she coming with us?" she asked, as she draped her arms around Lady Jane's neck. The horse was hitched to the back of the carriage.

"Sylvia said you had not been to the stables—and with good reason. I thought you might enjoy riding and spending time with Lady Jane this weekend."

"I would enjoy that. Thank you so much." Lucinda threw her arms around Aleister's neck and hugged him once again. Even though it was not proper, Aleister never reprimanded her for showing such an affectionate display in public. This, however, added fuel to the proverbial fire of gossip. Aleister didn't care.

They left Lady Kingston's and arrived at the cottage, where Ms. Poe was awaiting their arrival. Lucinda descended the carriage quickly and hugged Ms. Poe. They had become quite close over the months. This was also frowned upon by the socialites. Aleister did not mind this, either. He was quite close to Ms. Poe himself, and he was happy Lucinda had a female mother figure to go to.

They quickly settled in and had their evening meal together, enjoying one another's company and the intimacy of the cottage.

They also enjoyed their privacy in the bedroom at the cottage—not having to sneak around as they had to at Lady Kingston's.

After Aleister and Lucinda bid Ms. Poe goodnight, they made their way quickly to the bedroom. A week was much too long to be apart. Aleister took Lucinda in a way she had never known. It was almost as if he were a different man. He was ravenous and hungry for her. He had a need she felt could not be satisfied.

In the back of her mind, she wondered if the evil in the mansion had finally gotten to him. No matter how strange and frightening, Lucinda was terribly excited by Aleister's lovemaking that night.

No words were said afterward; they held each other and slept. They both slept more soundly than they had in quite a while.

In the morning, Lucinda awoke before Aleister. She watched him sleep, and she began thinking about everything—the night before, the murders, the attack in the stable, the attack from the judge, the evil in the mansion. Lucinda began to wonder if Aleister could be tied to the murders, if he had alibis for those nights. She had never asked him, because she knew he was not the murderer—he was far too kind and gentle.

He awoke and they talked for a while before getting up to begin their day. As they ate breakfast, Aleister inquired, "My dear, I think you are in need of more dresses, and maybe a few hats. Would you like to go into town and see what the newest fashions are? We can shop and dine, and maybe see a play. How does that sound? I think it's about time we show ourselves to London as an engaged couple, don't you?"

Lucinda had never thought about it before. She had been sequestered at Lady Kingston's, and had been distracted with the commotion and fear from the murders. They had not been out in London society since they had become engaged. They had actually never been in London together but once, and that was the day he had first met her.

Lucinda beamed with excitement. "Oh, Aleister, do you mean it? That would be wonderful. I have never really shopped before, or seen a play, or dined out. That sounds like so much fun."

"Very well, then. Be ready in one hour. I will send Ms. Poe up to help you."

Lucinda jumped up and kissed Aleister. When she turned to leave, he winked at her. She giggled and ran to their room. Ms. Poe was only a few minutes behind her.

Ms. Poe helped an excited Lucinda into her dress and helped her with her hair. She was ready in less than an hour. Dr. Wellington was impressed with her enthusiasm. They headed into town. Aleister took Lucinda into the most extravagant shops, and helped her decide what to purchase.

They were seen by many important people in town. Lucinda was proud to be on the arm of the handsome doctor. She hugged him and kissed him in public. He returned her show of affection. They found themselves in a hat shop, where they bumped into Melinda Whitman.

"Oh, Lucinda, you look simply radiant, my dear. How are you fairing at Lady Kingston's? I hear from Victoria that you two have become increasingly close."

Lucinda smiled and replied, "Yes, Mrs. Whitman. We have become very close, and everyone knows it."

Mrs. Whitman looked very sad as she recalled having to reprimand the girls for being too playful in the presence of the judge. "You, know I only did what I thought was best for you both when you were younger, don't you?"

"Oh, Mrs. Whitman, I did not mean to offend you. I know you did your best to protect me. I only meant that, with no restraints, Victoria and I have become the best of friends."

Just then, Lucinda heard the gruff voice of a man she desperately hated. "Ah, Melinda, there you are. We most go, if you are determined to go that confounded play."

Since Lucinda and Aleister had their backs to the judge, he did not know with whom his wife was conversing.

Lucinda and Aleister turned to face the judge. Even though Lucinda knew she was safe with Aleister, she still had an uneasy feeling having the judge to her back. Lucinda did not speak, but Aleister did.

"Judge Whitman."

"Dr Wellington, I did not recognize you from behind." Judge Whitman was getting upset. His face began to flush, and he talked through clenched teeth. "I am not sure I have seen you since your announcement at Lady Kingston's— congratulations are in order. I must say, I was surprised that you would take one of your staff as your wife."

"Oh, you are mistaken."

Lucinda's heart dropped. She thought, *Is he denying me in front of the judge? Why would he do that? I thought he loved me.*

Aleister continued. "Lucinda was never a member of my staff. She was one of yours, and I was her benefactor. I always saw more than a servant girl. To me, she is a queen—a queen who was shackled and abused."

The judge's anger quickly became apparent to everyone. "Now, you listen here. She was never abused in my house!"

"Well, judge, no one accused you of anything. I found her on the streets, beaten and bloody. I never said who attacked her."

"'Attacked!' So it's gone from 'abused' to 'attacked'! Just what are you insinuating, doctor?"

Melinda could take no more. Without warning, she burst out in anger at Judge Whitman. "Oh, don't be so pious. We all know what happened the night Lucinda ran away! You attacked her and tried to have your way with her!" Melinda's words echoed throughout the hat shop.

The judge slapped his wife without hesitation. "You

have no right to speak to me that way—no right to accuse me of something like that!" He grabbed Melinda by the arm and pulled her so hard she almost fell. She struggled against him.

Lucinda looked pleadingly at Aleister.

Aleister grabbed hold of the judge's fat hand squeezing into the flesh of Melinda Whitman. "Judge, I don't think she wishes to leave with you."

Judge Whitman was outraged. He threw his wife to the floor and took a swing at Dr. Wellington. Aleister ducked; the judge missed. While the two men were grappling, Lucinda rushed to Melinda's side. The two women watched as the men continued to battle, though the scuffle did not last long. Aleister finally pummeled the judge in the face. It didn't take much to make the judge retreat.

"You'll pay for this, Wellington!" the judge shouted. He then looked down at the floor, where his wife was still sitting. "And you, bitch, do not step foot back in my house!" He then gave Lucinda a piece of his mind. "And as for you, you dirty whore, I hope Jack the Ripper makes you his next victim!" Then he turned and stormed out.

With that, Aleister jumped at the judge, ready to rip his throat out.

Lucinda ran to him quickly; she and held tight to his arm, pleading, "Aleister, no. Let him go. Please."

Lucinda's voice quieted Aleister. She had a way about her that made him bend to her will. "Come ladies. Let's dine, shop, and see a play."

Melinda looked fearful. She knew no one would take her in, because everyone feared her husband. Both Lucinda and Aleister could tell she was very upset.

"Mrs. Whitman, you will stay at my house. I would not leave you to the streets."

Melinda Whitman immediately broke into tears. "Oh, Dr. Wellington, you are too kind."

As kind as he was, Lucinda felt guilty asking one more favor of him. She knew how close Melinda Whitman and her servant Loraine were, and she knew Judge Whitman would take his anger out on Loraine.

Aleister could tell by the look on Lucinda's face that something was troubling her.

"What is it, Lucinda. Mrs. Whitman will be safe at the mansion."

Lucinda confessed, "I know, it's just that—"

"It's just what?"

"It's Mrs. Whitman's servant, Loraine." When Lucinda mentioned Loraine's name, Melinda's eyes filled with tears, and she looked like she was fearful for her own life.

Aleister said, "I understand. I will send for her immediately and she, too, can find refuge at my home."

Lucinda felt relieved. She loved him for his kindness. Melinda Whitman had a great sense of ease, one she had not felt throughout her entire marriage. She felt free, finally. The three spent the afternoon together. They all had a nice day, regardless of earlier events. At the end of the day, they stopped by the Whitman house to pick up Loraine. Then Dr. Wellington instructed the coachman to go to the mansion.

It was the first time Lucinda had been there since she had asked Dr. Wellington to leave with her. An eerie feeling came over her. She felt as though she were being watched— like something was standing so close to her, it was brushing up against her. She was anxious to leave.

They got Melinda and Loraine settled into their rooms. Lucinda and Aleister explained that they do not stay there when Lucinda visits Aleister. They explained that Lucinda is uncomfortable in the house, and that they stay in his cottage.

As they turned to leave, Aleister warned Melinda about the house. "Mrs. Whitman, I have one firm rule in this house. It may seem strange to you, but it is for your own good. You can ask any of the staff and they will tell you the same. You must keep your bedroom doors locked at night, and you must not come out until daybreak. Can you abide by this house rule?"

Melinda looked at Lucinda, as if to silently ask if he was jesting.

Lucinda responded, "Please, Mrs. Whitman, do this one thing. There is a very good reason I do not stay here."

Melinda wanted to inquire further, but was just grateful for Dr. Wellington's hospitality. And it was peculiar that Lucinda would not stay in the house, so there must be a reason for it. She agreed to the doctor's request. Melinda and Loraine retired early, just after Dr. Wellington and Lucinda left.

Aleister and Lucinda went straight to the cottage for the night. It was a tiresome day, so they went directly to bed and fell asleep almost immediately. They both slept soundly.

However, not everyone in London was safely tucked away in their beds, behind locked doors. Another murder occurred that night. It was not thought to be at the hands of Jack the Ripper. A homeless man was beaten to death, in much the same manner as the stable hand. His clothes were the only thing that led the inspectors to believe he was homeless. The identity of the man was not revealed; there was no way to determine who he was. His head was crushed, making him unrecognizable.

Inspector Anderson recognized the brutality of the murder, and knew in an instant that it was committed by the same person who murdered the stable hand, Roy. He went to the commissioner with his suspicions. The commissioner was outraged.

"Inspector Anderson, I have warned you about such speculations. When you investigate a murder, just conduct the investigation and close your case as quickly as possible so you can move on to more important cases. Conclude this case, and go about your business. I don't need your speculations coming to the public eye. The community is frightened enough by Jack the Ripper without you adding more fear."

"Yes, sir," Inspector Anderson said, and he turned to leave. He knew in his heart that the commissioner had his own suspicions about Jack the Ripper, and he was certain the commissioner thought all the murders were related. Inspector

Anderson knew deep down the commissioner was under pressure from someone higher up to conceal as much as possible from the public about Jack the Ripper.

Because of the heightened fear of the Jack the Ripper murders, news of any murder set the community of London on edge. It would not take long for news of the homeless man to spread, so Inspector Anderson wanted to inform Dr. Wellington and Lucinda. He wanted them to know firsthand what had happened, due to the similarities to the murder at Lady Kingston's.

Chapter 16

Aleister and Lucinda were engrossed in a game of chess, when they heard a knock at the door. Ms. Poe answered and ushered the inspector into the room. Aleister jumped to his feet, fearing that something had happened to Mrs. Whitman at his home.

"What is it, inspector? Is everything alright?"

"There has been another murder."

Aleister's heart dropped. He asked quietly, "Where?"

"Behind Bailey's Pub, in the alley."

"Another prostitute?" Lucinda asked.

"No. It was a homeless man."

"Do you think this murder is related to the rest?" Dr. Wellington asked.

"The murdered man was beaten like the stable hand."

"What was the man's name?" Lucinda asked.

"We don't know. His head was crushed into a million pieces. There is no way to tell for sure who he was."

Aleister asked, "So, is the stable hand's murder now

being investigated further?"

"No, Dr. Wellington. The commissioner wants this investigation concluded immediately, and does not want it connected. My hands are tied. I just wanted to let you know so you can be cautious."

"Thank you so much, inspector." Dr. Wellington said. They all bid each other farewell and went about the day as well as possible.

Melinda Whitman read about the latest murder in the newspaper that morning. She decided she needed to see her friend, James Lawrence. She got ready and left the mansion early. Dr. Wellington's coachman took her into town.

Melinda felt excited, knowing she was no longer bound by her marriage vows. She had just arrived outside the home of the one man she loved most in the world, James Lawrence. She no longer had any restraints to bind her. Melinda knocked on the door. James opened it, surprised to see her and concerned by the large bruise on her face.

"Melinda, come in. Are you alright?"

"I am more than alright. I am free."

"What?" He absentmindedly touched her bruised face.

Melinda told him the entire story. She told him of the confrontation with Judge Whitman, and how Dr. Wellington had allowed her to stay at his home.

Then, James Lawrence did something he had longed to do for many years, a guilty pleasure he had never given in to before. He pulled Melinda Whitman into his arms. He tipped her head back and kissed her deeply. She did not resist. Melinda felt like her clipped wings had been restored.

James asked if he should begin the paperwork for her divorce. She immediately answered "yes." She could see the light. Her life would finally be worth living. They spent a blissful afternoon together before Melinda returned to Dr. Wellington's home.

Lucinda returned to Lady Kingston's, and Aleister returned to his mansion.

Victoria was thrilled to see Lucinda. She had some wonderful news to share with Lucinda. "I am so happy to see you. I have been on pins and needles since this morning. I received a letter from my mother. She told me what happened Saturday and she said she went to see James Lawrence yesterday. She has begun divorce proceedings. She is finally free of my father. I was so fearful that she would die at his hands after a life of misery. You know it is thanks to you."

Lucinda wasn't sure how much Melinda had told her daughter, so she wasn't forthcoming with any information. "What do you mean?"

"If you and Dr. Wellington had not provided her a safe place to stay, she would not have left him."

"Well, I suppose that your gratitude should be directed to Aleister more than to me."

"Lucinda, you and I both know that, as generous as Dr. Wellington is, he would have never gotten in the middle of another family's affairs, had it not involved you. He did it out of love for you. So, thank you for whatever you said or did to entice him to help her." Victoria hugged Lucinda and seemed the happiest she had ever been.

They went about their week as usual. Headmistress Dalton was still exercising caution with students, never knowing when the next murder would occur, and fearing there might be another at the school.

Chapter 17

It had been almost a month since the last Ripper murder, and the community was beginning to feel a little at ease, thinking it had ended. However, little did they know, there would soon be another victim.

Dr. Wellington had been able to procure more cadavers, and he experimented into the early hours of the mornings. Since the Ripper murders had subsided, Dr. Wellington's questionable associates were able to carry out their work. Dr. Wellington enjoyed getting back to his experiments. However, as much as he enjoyed his work after hours, he always anxiously awaited the weekends when he would be with Lucinda.

One night, while he was conducting experiments on one of his cadavers, the grave robbers brought Dr. Wellington a prize beyond compare—or so they thought. An unexpected knock came at his door. He was startled. He wasn't expecting his associates, since they had visited him just the night before. He reluctantly walked to the door and, almost in a whisper, asked, "Who's there?"

A familiar voice came back in response. It was the voice of one of the grave robbers. "Let us in, quickly."

He opened the door. "What is it? I wasn't expecting you back so soon."

"We have something we thought you might like. We have been watching this one for a couple of weeks. It has been under investigation, so it has been preserved with formaldehyde. We thought you might like it." They brought in a corpse wrapped in a large cloth. The smell of formaldehyde was overpowering. They laid it upon a table.

"Who is it?"

One of the men pulled the cloth away from the face of the corpse. Dr. Wellington was stunned. "This is Elizabeth Stride, one of Jack the Ripper's victims! Why did you bring this here?"

"We thought that, with your work and all, you would like this one to examine, or whatever it is you do in here."

At first Dr. Wellington was upset by the presumption, and by having this corpse his lab. As he paced, trying to figure out what to do with the corpse, something odd came over him. He had never before entertained the thought. He was desperate to find out who was behind the murders, and now he had a Ripper victim in his lab. Who better to reveal the identity of Jack the Ripper than one of his victims? The decision was made.

"Here—take this and be off. Mention this to no one." He shoved money in the hands of one of the grave robbers, and ushered them out of his lab. He shut and bolted the door. He wrapped the corpse up tightly. He then headed to the mansion with fervor and determination.

Ms. Poe heard Dr. Wellington come into the house. He was rummaging around his study. She was concerned, so she went to check on him.

"Dr. Wellington, is everything alright? What are you looking for?"

"That book," Dr. Wellington responded, without looking up from his search.

"What book, sir?"

"The doctor who lived here before—his book."

"Oh, no. Not that book of abominations. Why would you need that?"

He stopped and briskly walked to Ms. Poe. He grabbed her by the arms and looked desperately into her eyes. "Ms. Poe, I have access to something that may shed light on this Ripper case. I need to know what his victims know, for

Lucinda's safety. Please help me find the book. Don't tell anyone what I just said to you, and don't tell anyone about the book. Please, Ms. Poe. It's for Lucinda."

"I hid it long ago. You're either lucky or damned that I didn't burn it, like I should have." She reached behind several books on a lower shelf and pulled out the old, decrepit book. Ms. Poe slowly and reluctantly handed it over to Dr. Wellington. "What are you going to do with that?"

"Ms. Poe, it's best you don't know. It's best you forget everything about tonight. Please." Without another word, he turned and left the house in haste.

Ms. Poe went back to bed. She had a bad feeling— nothing good could come of this. But her hands were tied. All she could do was pray.

Dr. Wellington was soon back at his lab. He unwrapped the corpse and retrieved the book from a bag. He sifted through the pages and finally found what he was looking for. It was a spell to revive the dead. He was distraught by the fact that he needed more than just a spell to recite. This incantation called for his blood, graveyard dirt and the nails from the victim's coffin.

Dr. Wellington fled back to the graveyard to retrieve

what he needed and was back at the lab in less than an hour.

Dr. Wellington had fear in the pit of his stomach, but he had to know if the corpses could remember anything about their murders. His morbid curiosity overwhelmed him.

The spell called for him to drive the nails into his hands like the wounds of Christ. Then he should let his blood drip onto the corpse. The graveyard dirt was to be scattered on the floor for Dr. Wellington to stand on while carrying out the spell.

Dr. Wellington took a handful of graveyard dirt and scattered it on the floor beside the table where the corpse lay and stood in it. He placed the dirty, old nails on a table with the head down and the tip up. He shoved first one hand and then the other onto the nails. It was a pain like he had never experienced before; he could not help but to scream out. He let the blood drip onto the corpse and then he recited the incantation.

The mutilated corpse of Elizabeth Stride began to twitch. He shuddered at the movement. Being a doctor, he had seen many gruesome things, but nothing could prepare him for he was about to witness.

The dead body began to gurgle and moan. It sat up. Its

eyes opened, and it looked around the room in confusion. It became frantic as its memories of its last moments of life came rushing back. It tried to get off the table to run away, but all it could do was flail about. Dr. Wellington took hold of the arms of Elizabeth Stride's corpse, in hopes of calming it down. He needed answers.

"Elizabeth, do you know what happened to you?"

The corpse nodded its head in response.

"Do you know who killed you?"

The corpse shook its head "no."

"Did you see the murder's face?"

Again, it shook its head "no." Then, with the increasing understanding that it was dead and brought back, the corpse began to get violent. It made a great deal of noise trying to get up from the table. It began to hit Dr. Wellington in order to make an escape. Dr. Wellington struggled with the corpse, but could not subdue it. Finally, he had no choice but to kill it once again. He picked up a scalpel and slashed it several times. He sliced the stitches on its neck, letting the wound open. When those efforts failed, he grabbed the book to search for another incantation that would stop it.

Dr. Wellington found it opposite the page of the incantation to revive the corpse. He did as it instructed. He pulled the two nails, still protruding his hands, out and shoved them into the eyes of the corpse. He recited the incantation and the corpse fell to the floor.

Dr. Wellington knew the body could not be discovered in his lab, so he cut it up and cast it into the stove to be burned. When he had cleaned up the lab and his wounds, he headed back to the mansion, exhausted. He slept late and missed most of his appointments that day.

Ms. Poe heard Dr. Wellington come home in the early morning hours. She knew he was tired, and she let him sleep in. She paced and worried about what he had done the night before.

Finally, just before noon, she heard him stir. He came from his room, disheveled and tired. He quietly sat and had his breakfast. It was obvious something had happened that caused a change in Dr. Wellington. He appeared anxious and nervous.

Ms. Poe could take it no longer. "Dr. Wellington, is everything alright? Did things go well last night? Where is that confounded book?"

He slowly and deliberately placed his spoon on his plate. He leaned back in his chair and wiped his mouth with his napkin. He looked at Ms. Poe with serious, but sad, eyes. She thought for sure she was going to be reprimanded for overstepping her bounds.

"Ms. Poe, if it were anyone else being so inquisitive in my private affairs, I would surely dismiss them. However, since it's you—why don't you have a seat?" He gestured toward a chair adjacent to him.

Ms. Poe sat; it was then that she noticed the bandages on his hands. She wanted to ask what happened to them but at the same time she did not want to know. She quietly said, "Dr. Wellington, I didn't mean to pry."

"I must have complete confidentiality."

"You know me, Dr. Wellington. I never repeat anything you say."

"I was brought a fresh specimen last night." He looked around to make certain no one was within hearing distance. He then whispered, "Elizabeth Stride."

Ms. Poe jumped up in shock. "Oh, no. Dr. Wellington! You didn't."

He grabbed her by the hand and gently pulled her back to her seat. "Ms. Poe, I had to know if the murder victims had seen their killer."

"And did she see? Could she tell you anything about the murderer at all?"

"No. She could tell me nothing."

"Where is the body now?"

"Gone."

"What do you mean gone, sir?"

"I had to dispose of it, so I incinerated it." Ms. Poe shook her head.

"That poor thing, having to die twice."

"It was never really alive the second time, Ms. Poe."

"It was aware, was it not?"

"Well, yes, I guess. It was no longer Elizabeth Stride. It was some dark creature. I will tell you this; I will never again use that book. I brought it in and put it back where you hid it. I can tell you, though, I now know the obsession the doctor had with the dead."

"He was an evil man, a necromancer. It is because of the terrible things he did here in this house that evil roams here. I am afraid you have opened that door further. Please be careful what you play with." Ms. Poe stood up and slowly walked to the door, wringing her hands. She stopped and turned to ask one more question, "Will we be spending the weekend at the cottage?"

"Yes. Nothing has changed."

"I think maybe you have." Ms. Poe turned and left the room.

Dr. Wellington finished his breakfast. He was deep in thought, pondering the things Ms. Poe had said. He knew the evil in the house was something the doctor had invited in with his practice of necromancy.

Dr. Wellington felt strange, but he couldn't put his finger on why. He couldn't decide if he was upset over the events from the night before, or if he was just very tired. But as the day wore on, he continued to feel odd. He was not himself. He felt irritable and easily unnerved by the staff. This was uncharacteristic of Dr. Wellington. Everyone in the house avoided his company, including Melinda Whitman.

His demeanor continued to be strange for the rest of

the week and his hands healed remarkably fast—within two days. Friday came, and he sent Ms. Poe to the cottage as he went to retrieve Lucinda from Lady Kingston's. When he arrived, he was greeted by his cousin, who was very surprised at his appearance.

"Cousin, you look as if you haven't slept in days." She reached over and patted his stomach playfully. "Nor eaten. Is everything okay? Are you ill?"

"I'm fine. I have just been working a lot this week. That's all." His excuse wasn't very convincing, but Sylvia did not press him for an answer.

"I think Lucinda is ready to go. She has been waiting on you. Come in, and I will send for her."

"Thank you, Sylvia." He walked into the parlor and took a seat on a large sofa. He hadn't rested well that week. He felt as if something was residing in his body. It was a very troubling. He felt sure he had let some spirit have access to him. He hadn't been able to talk to Ms. Poe about it; their relationship had been strained because she disapproved his use of the book. Dr. Wellington was thrilled to have Lucinda to talk to. He knew she would not judge him. Aleister Wellington laid his head back and closed his eyes—he hadn't felt so at ease all week.

Lucinda walked into the room and saw him sitting, looking so dreadful. She slowly and quietly walked over to him, examining his appearance.

"Aleister," she said, as she knelt down just in front of him. Lucinda reached over and touched his hand.

His eyes slowly opened. "Ah, sweet, sweet Lucinda. How wonderful it is to see your shining smile. It has been a long and troubling week."

"What has happened? Are you alright?"

"I will explain everything when we are settled in at the cottage. Come now, let's be off." He smiled wearily.

Lucinda took Aleister by the hand and walked out with him. They bumped into Sylvia on the way out.

"Lucinda, take good care of my cousin this weekend." She smiled at Lucinda. "And cousin, get some rest this weekend." She leaned over and kissed Aleister on the cheek.

He kissed her cheek, as well. "I will, cousin."

Lucinda and Aleister left and stepped into the carriage awaiting them. It wasn't long before they arrived at the little cottage in the woods. They entered to find Ms. Poe preparing dinner. She gave Aleister a disapproving look. She walked to

Lucinda and took her hand. "It is so good to see you. How was your week?"

"It was good. How was yours?"

"Not so good. But I hope the weekend will be better." Lucinda could easily see the tension between Ms. Poe and Aleister. Exasperated, she demanded, "What is going on? What happened this week?"

"I will let Dr. Wellington inform you." Ms. Poe turned and walked away.

Lucinda looked at Aleister, "Well?"

"Ms. Poe, will you let us know when dinner is served? I will enlighten Lucinda of the past weeks events."

"All of them, sir?" Ms. Poe asked smugly.

"Yes, Ms. Poe, all events." Aleister took Lucinda by the hand and took her into the parlor. "Lucinda, this is probably going to be very hard to hear. Please do not judge me too harshly. I have a good reason for what I did." He reached over and took her hands in his.

Lucinda became very frightened. She could not imagine what he was about to disclose. "My dear Aleister, who am I to judge you? I am but a lowly servant girl who was rescued by a charming prince. But you are scaring me. What is it? What have you done?"

"It is nothing good." He paused for a moment to gather courage. "Do you remember the story I told you about the doctor who lived in the mansion before me?"

"Yes. How could I forget? It was because of him that I cannot stay in the mansion."

Aleister's head dropped, and Lucinda knew instantly he had done something terrible.

"Aleister. Tell me. I cannot stand the suspense."

"I was working late earlier in the week, and my associates brought me a specimen I was not expecting. I used an incantation from a book that belonged to the necromancer, and it worked. The corpse was reanimated."

Lucinda looked as if she were going to be ill. Her voice got caught in her throat as she asked, "Why? What would possess you to use that book?"

"I asked it questions about the Ripper. I had to know. I thought, if I knew whom, I would discover why. And then I would know whether or not you were in danger."

"Why would you think this corpse could help?"

"It wasn't just any corpse."

Lucinda knew exactly what he meant. "Oh, Aleister, please tell me it was not one of the victims."

"It was. It was Elizabeth Stride."

Lucinda became so sick she could not hold back. She turned her head and vomited.

Aleister held her hair back.

"Lucinda, are you alright? Please do not think badly of me. I am the same man. I still love you. I did this to make sure you would be safe."

Lucinda did not speak. She was vomiting with such violent heaves, she could not respond to Aleister. Ms. Poe heard Lucinda but wasn't sure what it was she was hearing. She rushed in to see what was the matter. She stopped short at the door in surprise.

"Lucinda! Is she alright? What is wrong?"

"I think she will be fine. I was telling her what I had done, but before I could finish her nerves took hold of her."

Lucinda looked at him and forced the heaving back for a moment. "What more is there? Is this not bad enough?"

"The rest of the story can wait." Aleister tried to avoid concluding the story of his actions.

"Tell me, or I will have the coachman take me back to Lady Kingston's," she demanded.

"The corpse was not controllable. I was able to get a few short answers before it became very active—actually, violent. I had to subdue it."

"It was a woman. By subdue, do you mean you killed her?"

"It was no longer a woman. It was not human. It was a monster, and I was defending myself. It attacked me. I had to put it down. I had no choice."

The subsiding shock allowed her to stop vomiting. Then sadness took over, and Lucinda sobbed as she tried to continue the conversation.

"How did you do it?"

"I grabbed a scalpel and sliced the stitches on its neck. When that didn't work, I shoved graveyard nails through its eyes and recited another incantation to end it. I then burnt it. I could not just leave it in the laboratory to be discovered. I had to dispose of it."

After his response, Lucinda stood up without saying a word; she walked out of the room and sat on the front porch. Aleister knew she would not take the story of his actions lightly, but he did not think she would be this upset. He leaned back in his chair with such a melancholy feeling. He was unsure what to expect of her next.

Ms. Poe didn't say anything, either. She went back to preparing dinner. She, too, was unsure of Lucinda's intentions.

Lucinda sat on the porch, amazed that Aleister could perform such a horrible act. She remembered when he had told her of his work with the cadavers; she knew it was to benefit medical science. However, the reanimation of Elizabeth Stride was almost more than she could bear. What he had done was an abomination. How could she love a man like that? What had he let into his soul by opening that portal?

But then, just when she thought she could no longer love him, she looked through the window into the parlor. There, just where she had left him hours earlier, he sat with his head in his hands. She could see he was broken. She knew he was not devastated by what he had done, but by her disappointment in him. Lucinda could tell that he was fearful of losing her.

Then she saw more than just a doctor performing research, but a man who had saved her—had taken her into his home and had loved her with all his heart. Then she no longer felt disappointed in him, but rather in herself. In her heart, she knew what he did was an attempt to protect her, not to be a monster. He would not have even opened that book, had it not been for her. She was the cause of his actions—she and she alone. Now, she felt guilty for so hastily judging Aleister.

Lucinda slowly stood up and dusted off her dress. Aleister heard the movement on the porch just outside the window. He looked to see her walking back toward to front door. He was anxious, unsure whether she was coming in to talk to him, or whether she was coming to pack her things and leave.

She slowly turned the doorknob and entered the house. Aleister wanted to run to her and hold her in his arms, but instead, he sat and waited to see what she planned to do. Lucinda walked into to parlor still fiddling with her dress as a distraction.

"Aleister," Lucinda said, so quiet her voice was almost inaudible. She knelt at Aleister's feet. "I love you."

"You love me, but?" he asked in a shaky, worried voice.

"But nothing. I love you. I don't want to speak of this again," she said, as she leaned over and kissed his gentle hands. Tears streamed down her face. She loved him so much, and could not bear the thought of losing him—no matter if he were Jack the Ripper himself.

Aleister was so relieved. He slid down from his seat and onto his knees in front of Lucinda. He pulled her in close and held her tightly. Then he cupped her face in his hands and kissed her passionately. "I love you, Lucinda. Please forgive me."

"I don't want to speak of this ever again, please."

"I have to know that you do not think me a monster, or I cannot go on with my life."

"I do not think that you are a monster, just a bit misguided. There is nothing to forgive. Now, can we leave this topic forever?"

"Yes." Aleister said as he kissed her lightly on the cheek. Aleister felt such relief that had he not lost Lucinda. He took her by the hands and helped her stand. He tried to distract from the subject by asking, "Are you hungry? I think dinner has been ready for a while now."

"I'm not very hungry, but I could eat a little something." She smiled sweetly at him.

They went into the dining room. It was so much smaller than the dining hall at the mansion or at Lady Kingston's, and Lucinda loved the intimacy of their meals there. Dr. Wellington rang the bell, and Ms. Poe brought out the food. Ms. Poe loved Aleister Wellington like a son, and even though she had been upset with him all week, she could not stay angry with him for very long. Seeing how sweet he was with Lucinda reminded her of what a good man he really was. She immediately melted. That evening, all was well.

Lucinda and Aleister retired early. The week had been much too long for them both. They walked into the bedroom, and Aleister slowly closed the door behind them. Anticipation was eating away at Lucinda. He put his hands around her waist and looked deeply into her eyes, as if he were peering directly into her soul. His eyes were piercing, unlike they had ever been before. She was both frightened and excited. The way he looked at her alone sparked the flame within her.

Aleister's kiss was heavy and deep. He kissed her with such fervor that she could not breathe. He pulled her in tighter against his hard body. She responded to his excitement. Lucinda gave in. Afterwards neither said anything. They simply fell asleep in one another's arms.

As the night passed, Lucinda began to have fretful sleep, with nightmares of the evil from the mansion invading her subconscious. She tossed and turned, and when she awoke, she could have sworn someone else was in the room with them. Lucinda sat up in bed, trying to discern the unseen presence to no avail. It was a futile effort.

Aleister awoke from Lucinda's stirring. "What is it? Is everything alright?" He touched her lightly on the arm.

Lucinda turned to look into his eyes—the eyes of the gentle man who had saved her from the streets of London—the man who loved her beyond compare. "I just had a nightmare. But—" she stopped short.

"'But' what?"

"Well, when I awoke, I was sure someone was in here with us, watching us sleep. But I couldn't see anyone. I guess it was just the nightmare. I'm fine, really."

Aleister pulled Lucinda back down close to him. Their bodies pressed together, their arms and legs sweetly entangled.

The rest of the night was peaceful, and the weekend was blissful. Everything seemed right with the world. But then, Lucinda returned to Lady Kingston's and Aleister returned back to mansion. Things were not all right with the world in reality.

Chapter 18

The first night back at Lady Kingston's, Lucinda had another dream of a prostitute being murdered in the streets. The woman's body was brutally mutilated by a monster disguised as a person. Lucinda could see every detail in his work. She witnessed the murderer slice through the woman's throat, exposing what was once under flesh, as blood flowed freely down the woman's breasts.

Lucinda could hear the gurgling sound as the woman gasped for one last bit of air, desperately clinging to every last second of life. Then it was over. The woman was limp and silent.

Lucinda watched on in horror, too terror-stricken to look away or run. The man went to work, cutting at the flesh of the corpse with deliberation. He pulled the organs out and placed them around the body. At one point, he wiped his brow with the back of his hand, as if exhausted from working on something very important. Lucinda thought it was strange, as if the murder actually had a purpose for the murderer—for Jack the Ripper.

When he was finished, he stood and tossed a small bunch of grapes on the woman, then turned to stare Lucinda in the face. It was dark, and all she could make out were piercing eyes. She awoke in a cold sweat.

Victoria—still sharing a room with Lucinda, per the headmistress' orders—awoke immediately, sensing that Lucinda was stirring. "What is it? Another nightmare about Dr. Wellington's house?"

"No. I dreamt of a Ripper murder. It was a new one."

"Lucinda, it's just a nightmare. Now, lay back and rest."

Lucinda lay back, but did not go back to sleep. She couldn't sleep for the rest of the night.

Morning came, and the two girls dressed for breakfast and went to the dining hall. Headmistress Dalton was sitting at the head of the table with a troubled look upon her face. It was a look the students were too familiar with. In her hands, she held a letter. They all knew what was to be said before she even spoke.

"Girls, can I please have your attention?"

They all immediately quieted.

"I have received another note from Inspector Anderson. There has been another murder in Whitechapel. It occurred last night. It was another prostitute. Her name was Mary Kelly."

"When did this murder occur?" Lucinda questioned the headmistress.

"Last night."

Lucinda and Victoria looked at one another. Lucinda couldn't believe she had once again dreamt of an actual murder.

Sylvia Dalton saw the strange look on their faces. "Lucinda, Victoria, may I speak with you two privately?"

They followed her out into the hallway.

"What do you know of this?"

"Only that I had another dream," Lucinda confessed.

"I thought as much. Could you tell anything about the murderer?"

"No."

"Okay, just try to go on with your day. There is nothing we could have done, anyway. And girls, please keep this to yourselves."

"Yes, ma'am," they responded in unison.

The days and weeks passed with no further murders. It

appeared that Jack the Ripper had concluded his violent acts for some reason. After a couple of months with no murders, things went back to normal at the school, in London, and with Lucinda and Aleister. His extra nightly work eventually completely subsided; he was so distracted by Lucinda and their wonderful love affair.

He and Lucinda finally set a date for their wedding. It was to be held that summer—the summer of 1889. Preparations were made by Aleister, Lucinda, and Ms. Poe. Melinda Whitman was still living at Aleister Wellington's mansion while her divorce was finalized. She also helped with the wedding plans.

Melinda Whitman was being pursued by James Lawrence. Their affair was a secret to no one, including Judge Whitman. They had plans of marriage themselves, after her divorce was final in a few months.

Judge Whitman continued to be a brutal and horrible man. However, the brutality he had inflicted upon his wife months before had been long forgotten. He continued to work as usual.

One day, while Melinda Whitman and James Lawrence were running errands in preparation for Lucinda and Aleister's wedding, they bumped into the judge in a cake shop. Melinda had not seen the judge since the day she left his home with her servant, Loraine.

The judge's face turned red and his veins bulged. Melinda had seen this face many times, just before a violent rage. She was so thankful that, this time, she was not alone with him. This time he could not take his anger out on her.

Judge Whitman walked directly up to James Lawrence. "You are nothing but a thief. You stole my wife right from under my own nose."

James responded, "Your wife, good judge, left you long ago, emotionally. I was just the one who was there to actually love and respect her."

"She is nothing better than one of the whores from Whitechapel, having relations with another man while she is still a married woman." He spat in Melinda's face.

Blind rage filled James. He attacked the judge, beating him severely. James left the judge with a broken nose, a black, eye, a bloodied mouth, several cuts to the face and head, and many bruises. The attack was so quick and unpredicted, the judge had no time to react—not that he could, as fat as he was. James was lean, fit, and quick. Judge Whitman had insulted the wrong person that day.

"And Judge Whitman, Melinda is a lady. She never came to me when you were married—it was only after she was free from you that she came to me. What's more, she will forever be treated with the love and respect a woman deserves. If you ever touch her, come near her, speak to her, or even speak of her, I will kill you." James took Melinda by the hand and led her away.

Melinda said, "Oh, James, do you know what you have just done? He has many friends in high places. They will surely arrest you for assault."

"Only if they have witnesses. If no one in the store wishes to get involved, there is nothing the police can do."

"Surely they will tell the police what they saw. They won't want to go against Isaiah."

"Melinda, you underestimate how badly your husband has tortured the citizens of London. I would not be surprised if no one says a thing."

"I hope you are right."

The two went about their day. Melinda loved that a man actually defended her honor, rather than beating her down. She had never had anyone be so protective of her before. She knew for sure after James defended her in such a manner—putting himself at great risk by attacking the judge—that he truly loved her. However, she had known James for many years, and she had never seen him become so enraged or lose his temper in such a way. She had never known him to hurt anyone or anything before. He had never even swatted at a dog before. He was always so kind and gentle. She wondered where that outburst had some from—obviously passion.

The judge wasted no time going to the police station to file a complaint. The investigator just happened to be Inspector Anderson. "How can I help you today, Judge Whitman?"

"I need for you to arrest a man who just assaulted me."

"It looks like he was pretty upset. Who was this man?"

"James Lawrence."

"The attorney, James Lawrence?"

"Yes, one in the same."

"Are you certain of this? I have known James since childhood, and I have never known him to attack anyone."

"Yes, I am certain of my attacker! I have witnesses, too! We were in the cake shop. You can go and ask and begin your investigation. Then you can arrest that maniac."

"Alright. Let's not be hasty. Let me take your statement first. Then we I will head over to the cake shop."

Judge Whitman explained what had happened—every detail. He also told the inspector that James had threatened to kill him.

The inspector finished up the report. "Okay. That's all I need from you now. I will go to the cake shop and then proceed from there. I will get in touch with you tomorrow, after I have had a chance to speak to the witnesses, and to James and Melinda."

The judge stormed out, slamming the door behind him, rattling the windows. Everyone looked at one another. The inspector just smiled and shook his head. He collected the things and set out for the only cake shop in London. When he arrived, the only person there was the owner, who corroborated the judge's story. However, he added a little white lie. He said the judge had thrown the first blow, and that James was merely defending himself. He gave a list of people in the shop at the time of the incident.

The inspector spent the remainder of the day tracking down and getting statements from everyone on the list.

Everyone had basically the same story.

Everyone on that list had been mistreated and wronged by the judge in some manner. They all talked when the judge left and decided it was time for the judge to be taught a valuable lesson. So, they made sure their stories matched. After they had made their decision, the shop owner sent a note to James via one of his workers who was delivering a cake. James was thrilled to see that so many were willing to protect him from the judge and, in the process, teach the judge a lesson.

Inspector Anderson went to speak to James. Melinda was still with him. He received the same story from them as well. He thought something was a little strange, because there was no variation in the stories whatsoever, other than that of the judge. But he was not disappointed that there would be no case against James Lawrence.

When Inspector Anderson concluded his investigation, he went to see Judge Whitman at his office. The judge was sure the inspector was going to inform him that James was being held in a jail cell. But that is not the news he received. He was livid. His face contorted as usual. "I cannot believe your incompetence. Did you get statements from the other costumers, and the shop-keep?"

"Yes, sir. I filed them at the police station. Everyone said you threw the first blow, and that James was only defending himself. I cannot arrest a man for self-defense. You are lucky James did not want to press charges against you."

"He threatened me." Judge Whitman protested.

"And, I would say, with good reason. You attacked him."

"This is outrageous! I will speak to the commissioner first thing in the morning. Clear out your desk, inspector, because tomorrow you will no longer have a job."

Inspector Anderson smiled and said, "I will show myself out."

As the inspector walked from the room, he heard a loud crash. The judge had picked up a large crystal bowl and hurled it at the fireplace. Inspector Anderson smiled as he continued to the front door.

Chapter 19

Inspector Anderson went back to his office and, against the orders of the commissioner, decided to look over the Ripper cases, as well as the case of Emma Bronze and the stable hand. He knew these murders were all related. He could not turn his back on this, even though the commissioner had ordered him to. He had to know that what kind of monster could commit these horrific crimes and stop the killing.

The inspector looked at all of the evidence. He went through photographs of the victims. He read all the statements. He discovered that one person stood out above them all, yet his hands were tied to pursue this suspect. His gut instinct had told him, ever since the murder of Emma Bronze, who the murderer was. This person had means, motive, and opportunity for all victims.

This person seemed obsessed with Lucinda Belle. So, that would explain the murder at the stables. This person knew Emma Bronze personally. This person also had come into contact with all of the prostitutes, and the murderer must have known the homeless man.

The inspector felt helpless, certain he knew the identity of the Ripper, but forbidden from participating in the Ripper investigation. He had also been warned to leave the judge alone. The inspector had also seen the judge's brutality and rage firsthand; he was convinced of the judge's guilt. He sat at his desk, feeling hopeless. Even though this weighed heavily upon the inspector, he put the files away and put the murders in the back of his mind. He went about his job solving crimes and handling cases that political bureaucracy wasn't hindering.

....

The date of Aleister and Lucinda's wedding was quickly approaching. This also meant she would be coming home from Lady Kingston's. Lucinda knew she would either be forced to return to the mansion, or have to stay at the cottage alone. Aleister could not travel back and forth from his London office to see patients everyday—the cottage was a bit too far out. Lucinda desperately wanted to return to the cottage with Aleister rather than the mansion, but she could not ask that of him.

She pondered what she should do. Even after considering everything, she knew she must return to the mansion. Lucinda thought it might not be so bad. After all, Aleister had said activity at the mansion had almost completely ceased. She was also reminded that Victoria would be going to the mansion to stay with her mother until Melinda and James were wed. So she would have Victoria there, as well.

The more Lucinda thought about returning to the mansion with Aleister and Victoria, the more appealing the idea was until, finally, she had come to look forward to it. And it would not be permanent. Aleister had promised to sell the mansion and buy her a home of her own—one that she loved.

The day finally arrived; when the two girls would be leaving Lady Kingston's—Lucinda for good, since she would be a wife soon, and Victoria until the fall. Sylvia had grown very fond of Lucinda and was going to miss her terribly.

Aleister arrived early in the afternoon to collect Lucinda and her things. He was met at his carriage by Sylvia, who was all smiles.

"Ah, cousin. It is bittersweet to see you today. I always love your company, but you will be taking my sweet Lucinda away. I have grown quite fond of her. I can see how you fell in love with her. She is indeed a beautiful person. Come." She took him by the arm and led him into the gardens.

"It is always wonderful to see you as well, cousin. I am so happy you like Luicnda. You were always such an important person in my life. I know she is extremely fond of you. She will miss you."

"Well, she doesn't have to. She is welcome to come back anytime to volunteer or to visit. Besides, she will soon be my cousin, as well. I just feel terrible about the way her year began here."

"About that, have you heard anything from the inspector?"

"No. I think, to be honest, he has been restricted from information that could help him. He was convinced that the Ripper had a hand in the Roy's murder. But did you know the commissioner pulled him from the Ripper cases?"

"Yes. The inspector had said he would inform me of any new revelations in the case. I haven't heard from him in a few months. He still hasn't uncovered Emma's murderer." Aleister said, as he twisted and wrung his gloves.

"To be honest, I don't think these cases will ever be solved; the commissioner wants it that way."

"It appears so. Everyone knows the commissioner was only put in place to protect certain politicians from ever facing justice for their crimes."

"Well, dear cousin, do you ever speculate about the murders? Who do you think that it was?" Sylvia asked, as she put her hands on his.

"I really don't want to say."

"Aleister, anything you say I will never repeat. But if you don't want to share, I understand. However, I am a bit of a gossip and I am happy to share my thoughts with you. I believe it was Judge Whitman."

"I think you are correct, cousin. I still worry about Lucinda and wonder if he will one day complete what he began."

"I think, if it was the judge, he has been scared badly enough that he will avoid Lucinda. After all, no one would witness for him when he accused James Lawrence of attacking him. I think people fear the judge less and less. He is losing control and, therefore, power. I think Lucinda is safe from the judge. I just wish he had to face justice." Sylvia declared.

"We know he won't face it in the courts, but maybe

someday, divine retribution will step in."

"Well, Aleister, that sounds a little evil," Sylvia giggled. "Come, let's find your love."

They walked into the house together, where they found Lucinda and Victoria already packed and waiting.

"Oh, how it saddens my heart," Sylvia said, as she wiped away an imaginary tear from one eye.

"Oh, Headmistress Dalton, I will be back soon," Victoria said.

"I know dear, and I will be counting down the days."

"And I will soon be your cousin. As close as you and Aleister are, I'm certain you will see me plenty." Lucinda hugged Sylvia.

Sylvia smiled and hugged both girls. "Please, be safe and enjoy your time. I will miss you."

"Aren't you coming to the wedding?" Lucinda asked.

"Oh, yes. And I plan on staying a few days. I will see you both then."

Sylvia bid Aleister, Lucinda, and Victoria farewell as they climbed into Aleister's carriage and headed back to his home. The ride seemed to take forever for Lucinda. Even though she was sure she had nothing to fear in that house, she still began to feel anxious the closer she got to it.

It wasn't long before they arrived. The coachman pulled the carriage up to the front door, where the footman and a few other servants were waiting, along with Ms. Poe and Loraine. Melinda was also there, awaiting her daughter's arrival. There was laughter and tears of joy.

Victoria was shown to her room by Loraine. Melinda helped her unpack. It felt strange to Victoria to be in someone else's home, but it also felt very safe. She had never felt safe coming home before. It was a wonderful relief.

Ms. Poe got Lucinda's things settled in her room. Aleister and Lucinda took a walk in the gardens.

"Oh, I have really missed these gardens. I had forgotten how much." Lucinda glanced in the direction of the stables. "Is Lady Jane back here, or is she still at the cottage?"

"I had her brought back here for you."

Lucinda's eyes beamed with joy. "Can we go see her? I missed her while I was at Lady Kingston's."

"I know. But I thought that under the circumstances--"

Aleister trailed off with pain in his eyes.

Lucinda took his hand. "I'm fine. I am beyond that. But you're right, I would not have gone back to the stables even if she had stayed."

Aleister pulled her closely and kissed her, as if it were the last kiss. "I have arranged for a coming home party for you and Victoria. Actually, it is more like a masquerade ball, to make up for the last ball meant for you."

"Are you sure that's a good idea?" Lucinda laughed nervously.

"I think we will be just fine. I have asked the inspector to come and give some security."

"It sounds wonderful. When is it?"

"Tonight."

"Tonight? I am not prepared."

"You will be. We just need to get you into the house and get Ms. Poe to help you. Come now." Aleister pulled her by the hand in a playful gesture, and they ran into the house.

Melinda and Victoria were already preparing for the party. Loraine and a few other servants were helping them.

Ms. Poe and a few more servants helped Lucinda prepare. It wasn't long before the girls and Melinda were ready and guests began to arrive.

Aleister brought Lucinda his mother's necklace to wear. "Please wear this again. It is so lovely on you. I also brought your masque."

Lucinda had never seen such a lovely thing before in her life. The masque was covered in beautiful jewels—tiny rubies, diamonds, emeralds, and sapphires. "Oh, Aleister, it is spectacular," she said as she reached for it. Then she looked into his warm eyes and said, "I would be honored to wear your mother's necklace."

She turned away from him so he could clasp it around her neck. The emeralds sparkled under the candlelight and specks of green danced about Lucinda's neck.

"Are you ready to meet your guests?" He took her hand led her down the stairs and into the ballroom.

Everyone gasped when they caught sight of Lucinda. She looked like a goddess, Aleister thought. Lucinda was much different now than she was at the first ball. This time she stood tall and proud; she intermingled with the guest like the lady of the house would. Lucinda had acclimated to

Aleister's world quite well.

Lucinda, Aleister, Victoria, and Melinda mingled among the guests. However, after a while, Lucinda lost sight of Aleister and Victoria. Finally, she left the ballroom to search for them. She bumped into the inspector and asked him for his assistance. Together, they began their search.

Chapter 20

There were many guests wandering around the mansion that night. However, there was on uninvited guest on the prowl. Victoria had spotted him as soon as he walked into the ballroom. She knew him, even behind his masque. She knew he could easily be lured away from the others. If he knew who she was, he would follow her. Victoria lowered her masque to reveal her face to him. She left the room and he followed.

Victoria went through the kitchen to arm herself with a knife. She quickly slipped it into the sleeve of her dress without anyone noticing, not even the uninvited man following her. Out into the gardens and away from the mansion, she led him. He followed like a puppy. When Victoria had found the perfect secluded spot, she turned to face him.

"I had to see you. I could not believe you came here with your mother instead of coming home with me." He lowered his masque to reveal himself, but it was no surprise that it was her father.

"I could not stand your brutality any longer. I was so happy to hear that mother had left and found refuge here. I don't have to worry about what comes into my room at night here."

Judge Whitman reached out to grab her, but she was quicker. She pulled the knife from her sleeve and slashed his throat. He staggered back in shock. He held his throat in a futile attempt to stop the bleeding. Victoria pushed him down and straddled him with the knife over her head.

"I saw what you tried to do to Lucinda the night she ran away. How could do that to her, or to me, your own daughter? You are nothing but a monster, and you deserve to die like a monster. I saw you with Emma Bronze, and I saw you with those whores from Whitechapel. You have no scruples, no morals, no boundaries. You'll never again taste the forbidden fruit."

The judge could do nothing but look at her in shock as his life extinguished. Victoria took the knife high in the air and thrust it into his chest. She continued to slash at him, ripping him open.

"Victoria! What have you done?" Lucinda cried out.

Victoria ceased the mutilation of her father at the sound of the one person she loved like a sister. Inspector Anderson ran up to Victoria and took the knife from her. She stood up.

"I did it for you and Mother, Lucinda. I did it for me."

"Why?" Lucinda cried out.

Just then Aleister came running to Lucinda. He had returned to the ballroom from the kitchen to find her missing. "Oh, my God. What happened?"

Victoria continued to explain her actions. "I know what he tried to do to you the night you ran away. I saw him. I was so ashamed because I did not try to help you. I was so afraid of him. Where he had no success with his attack on you he did with me many times." She looked at Inspector Anderson. "And if you had done your job, I would not be the one exacting justice tonight. His good courts would be."

"What do you mean?" The inspector looked puzzled.

"Emma Bronze flaunted their affair in my mother's face by telling everyone. I killed her, hoping the police would think father had done it. When that didn't work, the prostitutes he had slept with had to be sacrificed. He convicted these women of crimes that he had participated in. I thought that, as each of these prostitutes were murdered, surely the police would suspect him and have enough to connect him to the murders. When that didn't happen, I had to take justice into my own hands. I could not come here to

London and risk him getting to me or to Lucinda again."

The inspector began to explain. "Your father was my number one suspect. But I was not allowed to work on the Ripper cases. He was being protected. Were you responsible for the Roy's death as well?"

"He was attacking Lucinda. I did not protect her from my father, but I was not afraid of the stable hand."

"Why not?" Lucinda asked.

"I'm not sure. The night I killed Emma Bronze, something came over me. It was something uncontrollable. The minute I stepped foot into this house, I felt a surge of anger, regret, rage and a need for retribution. I felt fearless and was no longer afraid to do what needed to be done."

Lucinda and Aleister both knew what Victoria was talking about. They knew it was the evil that dwelt in the mansion. It had found a home in Victoria, causing her to commit these unspeakable acts.

"Why not just kill the judge?" the inspector asked.

"I wanted him to suffer humiliation the way we had. I wanted him to be punished by the very courts he had corrupted. When that did not happen, I had to do something.

I love Lucinda." Victoria's eyes welled with tears.

Lucinda walked over and hugged her dear friend, her dress becoming stained with crimson from the blood on Victoria's clothes.

"And the vagrant?"

"That was me as well. One night while I was following one of the prostitutes he attacked me and tried to force himself upon me. I killed him in self-defense."

Aleister looked at the inspector in amazement. "What do you propose we do? If you take her in, they will hang her with no trial. The judge's reputation will still be protected in death. You know that as well as I do. However twisted her reasons, what Victoria did was to protect herself and Lucinda. No one murder was innocent of crimes. So, what do you propose inspector?"

Inspector Anderson paced back and forth, running his fingers through his hair out of frustration. Finally, he turned to Aleister, "I am charged with making certain justice is served. There is only one thing I can do. Since I could not get justice through the legal system, I will have it here tonight. We have to dispose of the corpse and never speak of this to anyone. Is that agreed?"

Lucinda was astonished. She could not believe what the inspector had just suggested. But she was so relieved. Victoria could not believe her ears. She had finally found an honorable man who would come to her protection. Aleister, too, was shocked by the inspector's decision. However, no one was more surprised at the inspector's response than he was himself.

"I have an idea." Aleister said. "We finish the dismemberment and feed him to the pigs. I think that is fitting don't you?"

The inspector did not have the stomach for this, so Aleister was appointed to carry out the deed. Once the judge was dismembered, the four of them dragged his body parts to Aleister's pigs, far from the house. Lucinda had not even noticed the pigs until just before she left for Lady Kingston's. They were obscured from view, so no one would ever notice anything strange until the body was completely gone.

The inspector thought about the irony of the judge who was such a pig being eaten by pigs. The Jack the Ripper cases were never solved and there were no more murders.

Ronda L. Caudill, PhD

The End

www.ingramcontent.com/pod-product-compliance
Lightning Source LLC
Chambersburg PA
CBHW061615170626
46811CB00001B/429